CHEROKEE CLAY

CHEROKEE PASSAGES BOOK ONE

CHEROKEE
CLAY

CHEROKEE PASSAGES BOOK ONE

REGINA
McLEMORE

FIFE
PRESS

an imprint of

YOUNG DRAGONS PRESS

OGHMA

CREATIVE MEDIA

Fife Press
An imprint of Oghma Creative Media, Inc.
2401 Beth Lane, Bentonville, Arkansas 72712

Library of Congress Cataloging-in-Publication Data

Names: McLemore Regina, author
Title: Cherokee Clay/Regina McLemore | Cherokee Passages #1
Description: First Edition | Bentonville: Fife, 2020
Identifiers: LCCN: 2020935337 | ISBN: 978-1-63373-578-1 (hardcover) |
ISBN: 978-1-63373-579-8 (trade paperback) | ISBN: 978-1-63373-580-4 (eBook)
BISAC: YOUNG ADULT FICTION/People & Places/United States/Native American
YOUNG ADULT FICTION/Historical/United States/19th Century
LC record available at: https://lccn.loc.gov/2020935337

Fife Press hardcover edition November, 2020

Cover & Interior Design by Casey W. Cowan
Editing by Cyndy Prasse Miller & Dennis Doty

This novel is dedicated to all of the women and men of my wonderful, diverse family. I want to honor the memory of my Cherokee ancestors, especially those who walked the Trail Where They Cried. Because of your bravery and strength, I live today to attempt to tell your story.

Of those in my living memory, I first want to honor Mary Elizabeth Clay Philpott, my paternal grandmother, whose life and Cherokee heritage inspired much of this book. My brother, Jimmie Joe Price, always said that I should write a book, and even though you didn't live to see me published, this book is for you and your son, James David Price, too. Last but not least, I can't overlook how much my husband Dennis McLemore's sharp eye for detail helped me avoid making several historical errors.

TABLE OF CONTENTS

ACKNOWLEDGEMENTS

I WANT TO THANK ALL of my relatives and friends who have been so supportive of my efforts to complete *Cherokee Clay* and see it published, especially Tahlequah Writers, the Stilwell Library Book Club, and the Adair County Historical and Genealogical Association. Of course, much credit is due to my friends and colleagues at Oghma Creative Media—Casey Cowan, Cyndy and Gil Miller, and Michael Frizell, to name a few.

Even though he is no longer with us, I want to thank Hastings Shade, former Deputy Chief of the Cherokee Nation and a descendant of the great Sequoyah. I was privileged to work with Hastings at Sequoyah High School over twenty years ago and shared my book ideas with him. He answered several questions I had about early Cherokee history and culture. *Wado*, Hastings.

I

BACK IN
THE OLD LAND

"RUN!"

Bluebird shot out of bed when she heard her mother's command. She snatched up the small quilt she was working on, stuffing it into a burlap bag. Automatically, she turned to run toward her mother. Then she remembered her mother's words.

"Don't stop for anything because there won't be time. Just grab your bag, put on your shawl and shoes, and run for the back door. When I shout for you to run, it means I have seen the soldiers riding to our home. Run to the cave and hide, and stay there for at least a week or even ten days."

She obeyed her mother and ran for the back door. Their huge dog, Yo-na, like his bear namesake, growled menacingly at the strange visitors. If he were loose, he could betray Bluebird by trying to follow her. But Mother had tied him up like she had done every morning for the last seven days, since her cousin had stopped by to tell them the bad news.

The morning of that fateful visit Mother woke up in an agitated state. Her troubled eyes scanned their small cabin as if searching for something or someone. Young Bluebird frowned and looked around the room but could see nothing amiss. "What's wrong, Mother? What are you looking for?"

"I dreamed a strange dream last night. First, I saw a little chickadee flying to our house. But then a group of crows attacked it and drove it from the sky. They surrounded our cabin in a thick cloud. Look out the window and tell me if you see any crows."

Bluebird peered through the glass of their only window. "I don't see any crows, but I see a man walking up the path to our house."

Mother gasped and put her hand on Bluebird's arm. "Tell me. Is he white or Indian?"

"He looks like an Indian."

"That's all right then. Open the door and ask him to come in."

Bluebird obeyed, and a middle-aged Cherokee greeted them. "Si-yo, cousins. Are you well?"

Mother returned his greeting and answered his question. "My legs get weaker every day, but Bluebird grows bigger and stronger. How are you and your family?"

"I am sorry to hear you are growing weaker. My wife and children are in good health, but I came to warn you of the bad time coming to all Cherokees."

Mother sighed deeply. "Now I will hear what my dream means. Cousin, you are the chickadee who brings me news, but I also dreamed of crows who drove you away and surrounded my house."

The dark-skinned man shook his head in amazement. "Your dream medicine is as strong as when we were children. I still remember when you told me to stay home one day. I didn't listen and broke my arm when I fell from my deer stand. I am not a dreamer like you, but I think I understand your dream. The crows are the soldiers and their friends who are coming to every Cherokee home to take us all away. That's why I came here today to take you home with me so you will be safe."

"Yes, the crows are the soldiers and the local men who help them. But if the soldiers are coming to all our homes, why would we be safer at your house?"

"Because we won't be in houses. We will hide in a cave with my wife's clan. My wife and children are already there. We will stay until the soldiers have left our area. Then we can all go back home. My wagon and horses are waiting at the bottom of your hill. I will help you walk there. Come."

Mother bowed her head and remained silent for several minutes, and she raised her head and shook it. "Thank you for asking, but this is too quick. I must study on it."

His dark eyes got large, and his tone grew urgent. "What is there to think about? The soldiers and other whites are coming to steal all that you have. They will capture you and Bluebird, and, when you are caught, you will never come home again. Listen to me. I heard many of our people have died in those bad places where they are keeping Cherokees. There are others who were so mistreated or so sick that they wish they could die. I know these things are true because my wife's sister married one of the traders who sells food to the soldiers for their prisoners. Please, you must come with me."

He laid his hand on her thin arm as if to compel her to follow him. She gently removed his hand and her lips smiled, but her eyes showed resolve. "Yes, I know what you say is true. My neighbor, the old man who has always lived at the bottom of the hill, left two weeks ago because his son came to get him. They came to my house before they left, and his son told me local men were driving Cherokees from their homes. They claim their land and possessions as their own. The greedy white men now have soldiers to help them take what is not theirs. I am grateful to you for thinking of us, Cousin, but your wife's clan is large, and I can't breathe in a small, crowded cave. I have extra food you can have to help feed those who are hiding. Bluebird will help you carry it to your wagon."

His eyes were sad as he took her mother's hand before he and Bluebird walked away, loaded down with sacks of flour, sugar, and cornmeal. He took Bluebird's hand and squeezed it, saying, "May the Creator keep you safe, little cousin," and drove away.

A few hours later Mother came up with her own plan. If it worked,

Bluebird would be safe, but her mother would be taken. Today was the day Mother's plan was activated.

EVEN THOUGH THE light was fading fast, Bluebird's quiet feet knew the way through the woods to the hill with the hidden cave. Her mind replayed their last conversation. "We are blessed to live in the foothills of the great mountains. You won't have to climb very high to get to our cave. It will keep you safe until the soldiers leave."

"I don't want to go alone. Why don't you hide with me?"

"You know that would be foolish. With my slow legs, I would help the soldiers catch you. No, Bird, you must go by yourself. That's what my dreams tell me. They will think I am the only one living here. I will go with them quietly to wherever they take me, but with my weak legs and lungs, I will soon be joining your father. My little bird will fly away from their cage. The soldiers don't know about our cave, and you will be safe there until they leave. Don't come out for a week or even ten days, though, because they may search our place for more Cherokees."

Choking back tears, Bird stayed close to the shadows of the trees in case the soldiers rode through the woods, but all she could hear and think about was the mournful sound of Yo-na, crying for his lost friends. What will happen to Yo-na? Have I left him enough food and water for him to survive until I come home and turn him loose? She had to quit crying and worrying and make it to the safety of the cave, so as the sun went down, she ran on and on until she finally arrived at the hill. The climb would be the hard part. That she couldn't do without a light. Once she cleared the woods, she rummaged in her sack until she found the lantern and matches her mother had insisted she pack. Taking a deep breath, she willed her trembling hands to be steady until the lantern was lit.

The climb seemed to take hours, and once she almost stumbled, but Bird grabbed a small sapling as her feet slid and pulled herself back to an upright position. Finally, she reached the place where the entrance should be. Now where was that cave opening? It was small, but she should be able to find it. Bird shone the lantern over the rock surface. *There it is. Now I have to squeeze myself inside.*

LABORIOUSLY, BIRD SHOVED herself, the lantern, and her bag into the small opening. Almost falling, she caught herself before she dropped the lantern on the cave floor. That was close! She had to be more careful. She couldn't afford to break her only source of light. Bird shone the light around the cave, checking for spiders and snakes. Soon she would have to blow it out, and she dreaded that thought. The darkness in the cave would be absolute, and she was afraid of what might be hiding in wait for her. She thought of what her father, Path Finder, had told her before he died, when she was just a small girl.

"Bird, don't be afraid of the dark. There is nothing there that wasn't there when you saw it in the daytime."

There is nothing here to be afraid of. I have already checked the cave, and it is safe. All I need to do is wrap myself up and go to sleep.

Bird tried to be brave as she covered herself with the shawl, quilts, and blankets she had placed in the cave in preparation for this night, but her mind wouldn't obey. Her thoughts kept going to her mother.

What is happening to Mother? Did the soldiers hurt her? Will I ever see her again?

Bird's eyes flooded with hot, salty tears, and sobs soon wracked her small body.

No, I mustn't cry! I must be strong. Mother always said that crying didn't change anything.

Bird wiped away her tears and thought of happier things. In just a few days she would go back to her home and see Yo-na. Mother wouldn't like it, but she planned on letting Yo-na sleep in the house with her. That way she wouldn't be so afraid. But what would happen when winter came, and her food ran low? Mother said to leave before that happened. Bird had an uncle who had married a white woman, living in town.

"Go to my brother. He will take you in and keep you safe. It's a long walk to town, and I can't make it anymore, but you can. I should have sent you to him before, but I was afraid some white man or soldier would snatch you off the road and carry you away. Wait a few weeks, and they will be finished carrying off Cherokees from here and will go somewhere else. Then you can visit your uncle. His white wife's father lives with them, and he will not allow the soldiers to take his son-in-law. You will be safe in their house."

Bird comforted herself with these words as she pulled the shawl and heavy blankets around her body and struggled to go to sleep.

It was so dark. Bird missed her mother. How could she stand being in a dark hole for so long? Maybe she would leave tomorrow, find some soldiers, and surrender. *No, that was not what Mother told me to do, and I must be strong. Mother always said the women in her family are strong. I will not shame them.* In the morning, there would be a little light, and she could light the lantern for a while. She could walk around the cave, eat, and maybe even sew a bit. In the morning, things would be better.

Bird finally fell into a fitful sleep filled with nightmare images. Huge bat wings fluttered against the cave's ceiling. The giant bat lowered itself until it loomed over her sleeping form. The dream filled her with terror, and her throbbing heart awakened her. Bird tried to calm herself and slow her racing heart.

It was only a dream, foolish girl. There are no giant bats in this cave. Time to go to sleep.

Once, she thought her mother was lying beside her and quickly reached out to embrace the sleeping form. But she only found an empty crumpled blanket. Tears streamed from her eyes, and despair filled her heart until she was drowning in it. Finally, Bird rose above the despair.

No, I will not give in. If I do, I will die in this cave. Then somehow my mother will know I threw away the chance she gave me, and she will be ashamed of me. Besides who will feed Yo-na?

Bird welcomed dreamless sleep.

EARLY THE NEXT morning, she awoke in the darkness and wondered what time it was, then realized time didn't matter anymore. There was no one to talk to and no chores to do. How was she going to fill all the empty hours until she could go home again? At least she had plenty of matches and oil for her lantern.

Disentangling herself from her covers, Bird reached for the lantern and matches. She had kept them close to her so she could find them in the darkness. She carefully lit the lantern, slipped on her shoes, and made her way to the mouth of the cave. There was enough faint daylight streaming through to let her know it was daybreak. Now she could climb down the hill and look for a place in the woods to relieve her full bladder.

After she finished, Bird looked around, taking in the sights, sounds, and smells of the creatures that lived in the woods. She longed to linger and enjoy their company, but she remembered her mother's words.

"Now don't think you can stay in the woods and play. The soldiers might still be around and see you there, or some white man might be hunting and decide you need to be turned over to the soldiers. Then they will catch you and carry you off. Go right back in the cave and spend most of your time there. That way you'll be safe."

Obediently, Bird climbed back up the hill to the cave's entrance and picked up the lantern she had left close by. She walked back into the darkness looking for something to eat. She wasn't thirsty because she had taken a good drink from the small stream that ran through the woods, but her stomach grumbled for food.

After a light meal of cured venison and cold biscuits, Bird worked on the small quilt she had brought to the cave. When she finished, she would have a pretty, colorful child's quilt. Mother said her brother's young wife was expecting the last time she had talked to him, over a year ago. The quilt would be a gift for their young child. Bird sewed colorful patches together most of the day, taking time out for meals and stretches. She wanted to go out once more before the daylight faded to take care of her bodily needs. Her mother said she could use a corner of the cave if she had to, but if she were to stay in the cave for days, the stench might become unbearable.

Bird climbed down the hill and crept into the woods. While drinking and washing herself in the small stream at the foot of the mountain, she noticed a pretty stone shining in the stream and picked it up to keep. She was tempted to stay and enjoy the sunshine and the fresh air.

Can't I just stay in the light for a while longer? The cave is dark and scary. No, I will listen to Mother at least for today.

Five days and nights passed as Bird endured the darkness of the cave. Each trip to the woods lasted a little longer, and Bird didn't see signs of another human being. The morning of the sixth day, she decided to disobey. Yes, it was only the sixth day, but Yo-na was probably hungry. He may have even knocked over his water pot, and was dying of thirst. She needed to go back and see about him. He would be so glad to see her, and she couldn't wait to hug his big, shaggy neck. Maybe she would even let him into the cabin and into her bed. What a comfort it would be to sleep in her own bed with her faithful companion. She wouldn't have to light a fire, and she would stay close to the cabin so no one would know she was there. It would be perfectly safe, and she wouldn't be alone anymore.

WAITING UNTIL IT WAS almost dark, Bird crept silently through the woods, carrying her lantern and most of her supplies. Whatever she couldn't carry she would get early the next morning from the cave. Yo-na's joyous barks came to her long before she entered the clearing. It was just as she thought it would be. When Yo-na saw who it was, he emitted a strange whimpering sound, almost like human crying.

"Oh, Yo-na, I'm glad to see you, too! Did you think that I had left you? I would never leave my good boy. Let me get you loose."

Bird unhooked the long metal chain from the tree her mother had looped it around, and removed the other end from Yo-na's collar. The dog knocked her over in his enthusiasm.

"Hey, boy, calm down. I'm here now, and I'm not going to chain you up anymore." She reached out and hugged the dog's huge neck. "Now I have a surprise for you. You are going to come live with me in the house."

Yo-na hesitated at the open door. He had not been in the house since he was a small puppy.

"Come on now. It's all right. Come inside, and I will find you something to eat."

At the word "eat," the dog wagged his gigantic tail but still balked at entering. Finally, Bird grabbed him by his neck and tugged him through the doorway. Once he was through, he looked around nervously until Bird offered him a piece of dried venison. Yo-na gulped it down hungrily and looked at her with begging eyes.

"Here you go. Here's another piece, but that's all for tonight. We can't eat all our food up at once. It has to last for some time."

After making sure her favorite treasures were still where she left them, Bluebird added the small stone she had found in the stream to them. It was a reddish stone that had been polished smooth by the running water.

This will remind me of my time in the cave.

"I'm getting tired, Yo-na. Let's go to sleep."

But no amount of coaxing would make Yo-na get into bed with her, but Bird felt safe with him lying on a burlap bag next to her bed. For the first time in what seemed a long time, she had a restful night's sleep.

They continued their happy companionship for the next two days. Bird kept her promise about only venturing from the cabin under cover of night until one morning she awoke to a cool room. Such a cold snap reminded her that weather in the mountains was unpredictable. Fall and winter might come early this year. She had to prepare for the future. Should she gather wood and stay in the cabin, only lighting a fire at night to keep them warm, or should she do as her mother said and make her way to her uncle's house?

It is too soon to go there now. There might still be soldiers on the road and in town. Besides, what will I do with Yo-na? My uncle or his new family might not let me keep him, and I couldn't stand that. No, I will stay here through the rest of the summer and during fall and winter.

"COME ON, YO-NA. Let's go outside."

He wagged his tail and ran to the front door. Bird cautiously opened it and stepped onto the front porch. No one was around. It was just the two of them, and they were safe.

Bird laughed at Yo-na as he ran around the yard, like a pup, snapping at butterflies, relishing his freedom. She knew he was tired of being cooped up in the cabin. Bird grabbed a tow sack and walked to the backyard. She spent several minutes gathering small pieces of wood before Yo-na noticed she was gone and followed her. That would do for kindling for a while. She had some logs her mother kept in the smokehouse for building fires that she would put with it.

Suddenly, Yo-na's ears perked-up, and he growled.

"What's wrong, boy? Do you see a deer?"

White men's voices rang out. She dropped her wood and ran.

Yo-na charged back to the cabin. She had no doubt he fought bravely like the animal he was named after. His growls were aggressive, and she could imagine how he attacked the man, trying to protect her. She stifled her sobs at the sounds of the shot and his yelp, followed by the silence that meant her bear dog was gone.

I will be the quiet mouse they will never find.

Bird was hiding in the hollow of a big oak tree, biding her time until she could return to the house. Once she thought she heard a twig snap but decided it was just her imagination. Suddenly, Bird felt a sharp tug on her hair, and her heart stopped. The hunter had found his prey!

He yanked her out of the tree, dumping her onto the hard ground. She willed her trembling legs to run.

"What should I do with her, Lieutenant?"

Noticing the hunter had taken his eyes from her, Bird sprang up to make her escape, only to have a huge hand slap her back down to the ground. She must escape! Her cousin had told stories of what the soldiers and their helpers had done to Cherokees. First, they stole all of their belongings. Then they drove them from their homes and took them to evil places where many sickened and died. She had to escape. But how?

Another loud voice sounded. "Bring her to the cabin and tell her to pack a small bag for travel. You know Cherokee, don't you?"

"Sure do. But should we give them enough time to pack? Most of the time when it's the boys and me, we just put the guns to their backs and tell them to get out. That way they ain't got time to pull no tricks."

"I think you should be able to handle any trick that little girl can pull. She only looks to be ten or so."

The hunter sighed. "All right then just cause you say so. Girl, don't try to get away. I'm takin you back to your place for a short time. You can get a blanket, some clothes, and anything you don't mind carryin on a long walk. If I was you, I wouldn't get much."

Bird spat at him as he bound her hands with a rope. He laughed and squeezed her arm, hard. Back at the house, he untied her hands but stood beside her as she grabbed the bag, which had her special stone in it, and some more items from her cave stay. She put on her shawl and moccasins, grabbed a blanket in which she rolled up two changes of clothes, and added her extra socks and underwear. Bluebird blinked back tears as she turned to look at the only home she had ever known.

Her captor tied her hands again, jerked the rope that bound them, and helped her climb onto his horse.

II

BLUEBIRD

AND THE TRAIL

BIRD KNEW SEVERAL words of the white man's language and had understood most of the men's conversation. She had picked up their tongue from trading with the merchants in the town they visited on occasion. Bird was forced to learn so she could speak for her mother who refused to acknowledge English.

When they neared the town, she asked, "Stop here?"

Her captor, who had tied her securely to his saddlehorn, grinned. "I knew she understood. Lieutenant, she asked if we was stoppin here."

The lieutenant's cool blue eyes briefly lit on the unkempt man beside him and quickly looked away. "I have other business to attend to, so take her on to the stockade."

As soon as the lieutenant rode away, the bearded man leaned from his horse and spat out a large stream of tobacco. "Go on, Mister High and Mighty. I know you ain't got time to talk to the likes of me."

He paused to look at the trembling child. "Well, come on, girl. You'll be with your own people in a few minutes."

He rode a few yards, dismounted, and led Bird over to a soldier. "Here's another one for you. You'll need to watch her close. She's sly and knows more English than she lets on."

Bird tried to remember the English word for uncle but couldn't. She managed to point to the town. "Family here."

He untied her hands and spoke again in Cherokee. "Now, girl, I ain't got time to look up no lost relatives for you. You probably have family in the stockade. There are still some Cherokees in there, but the biggest part of them set off around a week or so. Here, go with this man. He will take care of you."

Bird clung to her former captor, pleading with him to help her.

He speaks my language. Maybe I can make him understand that I must be taken to my uncle's house. I will die if I have to stay in this prison.

"Now get away with you, girl. I ain't got time for this!" He roughly shoved her into the other white man's arms.

Bird screamed and tried to kick the soldier. He grabbed her boney arms and pinned them to her sides.

"You were right, Murray. She's a wild one. Settle down, girl!"

"Told you. Good luck. I'm goin home for supper."

The soldier half-carried her to the stockade, opened the gate, and shoved her in with her belongings. An elderly Cherokee woman with dancing dark eyes smiled at her and took her hand.

"It's all right, little one. You're with your own people now. What is your name?"

"My name is Bluebird, but my mother always calls me Bird. Is my mother still here? Her name is Lame Bird."

"I don't think she is here. They took most of our people around a week ago. They call us "the stragglers" because we are the ones who almost got away."

"I will still get away."

"Now you better forget about that. My grandson over there thought he could run away and look what they did to him."

Bird grimaced at the sight. A young dark-skinned man lay, beaten and unconscious, a few yards away.

"I doctored him the best I could, but he is going to be sore and bruised for a long time. Please put any thoughts of running away out of your mind."

Bird remained silent, but her spirit was speaking. At least he tried, but you should wait until you are walking with the others. It will be easier to slip into the woods then.

Bird spent the next week locked in the stockade. Rumors circulated that the soldiers were waiting for orders to begin the long march. She came to know the elderly woman and her grandson well. They were kind to her and having someone to talk to helped pass the long hours. There was even a connection of sorts.

"Grey Wolf, your grandmother said you are part of the Wolf clan that lives in what the whites call North Carolina. We live just a few miles from there on the border of North Carolina in the place they call Georgia. I have heard of your people."

"Yes. Our clan has lived there for many years. And we would still be there if I hadn't listened to Grandmother. We would be safe in the caves we always stay in when there is trouble with the whites. But no, we had to come and check on my uncle. He wasn't even home. And now we are caught by these white dogs, but we will not stay caught. I almost got away, and next time, I will!"

"Yes, you ran to escape, and look what happened to you."

Grey Wolf frowned at her. "Grandmother, you know I had to try. If I had made it, I would have found other clan members hiding in the caves. Then we would have come back, killed the whites, and let all of the Cherokees loose!"

"Foolish boy, if you had succeeded, the whites would have killed you and the family members you brought with you. Don't you see all of the soldiers and their guns? No, it's better that you didn't get away. I couldn't stand losing another loved one to an early grave." Grandmother paused to wipe a tear from her eye. "Now, little one, let's talk about you. What clan are you?"

"My mother always said we are of the Bird clan, but we never went around them. I was born in North Carolina, but my father moved us to where we live now when I was just small. I don't remember anything about it. Then my father died, and it's just been my mother and me for the last three years. We don't have any relatives except for a few cousins who live in North Carolina and my uncle who lives in town with his wife, a white woman, and her father."

Grey Wolf scowled. "In my clan, marrying a white is a disgrace. It sounds like you don't even have a clan."

"Now, Grey Wolf. Bluebird is a good Cherokee girl, even if she doesn't know much about her clan."

"Thank you, Grandmother. May I call you that? I have never had a grandmother."

Grey Wolf spoke up. "If you get to call her 'grandmother,' I get to call you 'Blue.' Sounds better than Bluebird or Bird."

Grandmother ignored him. "Of course, you can, child. I always wanted a granddaughter, but I only have this stubborn grandson."

Grey muttered something in Cherokee and stalked away.

"Grandmother, I am sorry I caused an argument between you and Grey Wolf."

Grandmother patted her back. "You didn't cause anything. This argument has been going on for a long time and isn't over yet."

TWO WEEKS PASSED slowly, and every day more Cherokees were brought in, and the stockade became filthier and more crowded. Blue joined Grandmother in comforting the distraught mothers and daughters. Once a small child was brought in by herself.

"Poor baby! Who will take care of her, Grandmother?"

"We all will, Bluebird, but I heard someone has volunteered to raise her as a sister to their little girl."

Grandmother opened up her arms to the tiny girl. "Come here, baby, and sit on Grandmother's knees."

The child smiled shyly, hesitated for a minute, and settled down, contentedly, in Grandmother's lap. Her round eyes sparkled as she looked up at Blue and held out her tiny hand.

Blue took the baby's hand and kissed the little palm. "How sweet! Does she have a name? Please let me hold her."

"I think her new mother calls her A-wi-a-gi-na.. Wait just a minute. Let me enjoy her for a while. It makes me think of holding Grey Wolf's mother."

Blue couldn't resist touching the baby's soft black hair. "That's a good name for her. With those eyes, she looks like a little fawn. What happened to Grey's mother?"

"She died of a fever two years ago. That's one reason he is so bitter. He is sad because he misses his mother."

Tears suddenly filled Blue's eyes. She quickly brushed them away. "I miss my mother, too."

Grandmother gently patted Blue on the shoulder. "I know, but maybe you will see her when we get to the place where the soldiers are taking us. Here, you can hold the baby now."

Bluebird took the child from Grandmother and settled her on her lap so she could look into the baby's eyes. She tickled the little chin and was rewarded with a giggle. Blue laughed and turned back to Grandmother. "Do you think so? If I knew I would see her again, I wouldn't try to run away."

"You saw what happened to Grey because of that. He is still bruised and sore."

"I know, but my mother wanted me to stay with my uncle. If there was just some way to get word to him, he would come and get me."

Grandmother sighed and shook her head. "Bluebird, there is something I need to tell you. I talked to one of my friends who knows English, and he told the soldiers you have an uncle in town. The soldier said, 'Tell me his name, and I will arrest him, too.'"

"But Mother said his white father-in-law would protect him."

"Perhaps. But would a white man be willing to take a Cherokee girl into his household?"

"I don't know."

A-wi-a-gi-na suddenly cooed and waved her arms. Blue turned to see a smiling, plump middle-aged woman. The baby's adoptive mother, Grey Dove, laughed as she held out her arms. Following close behind her was a scowling little girl. "Give us our baby back!"

Blue raised her eyebrows in mock surprise. "You must be the big sister. Here, I'm not trying to take your baby." Blue handed the baby to her mother.

"Tsu-la! Don't be rude. No one is going to take your new sister. I am sorry for the way Tsu-la is acting."

Grandmother laughed and patted Tsu-la's cheek. "That's all right. She is just acting like her namesake. Foxes are protective mothers."

Tsu-la grinned at Grandmother. "And sisters, too."

"Yes, and sisters, too. Blue, give Tsu-la that piece of bread I kept from breakfast. Big sisters need to eat a lot so they can take care of their little sisters."

Tsu-la snatched the bread from Blue's hand and crammed it into her mouth. Her mother scolded her. "Tsu-la, don't eat like a starved gi-tli and say wa-do."

Tsu-la's lip trembled, and Blue teased to keep her from crying. "That's all right, Tsu-la. I have always loved puppies and dogs even if they gobble their food. My dog's name was Yo-na."

Tsu-la's dark eyes shone. "So do I. Father says I can have a puppy someday. "Wa-do for the bread. It was good."

Grandmother had been watching Blue's interaction with Tsu-la. "Tsu-la, why don't you and your mother and sister stay and talk with us? It is good to have friends even in a place like this."

Blue learned that Tsu-la and her mother were taken when her husband was away fishing. Blue saw tears in Grey Dove's eyes when she spoke of her husband, but she dried them and said, "I hope he got away. I just wish he had taken Tsu-la with him so they both could be free."

Grandmother commiserated with her. "Yes, we all have wishes. I wish Grey Wolf and I had stayed home instead of coming here to see my brother. If we had stayed at home, we would probably be hiding in the caves with our clan now."

"And I wish I had listened to Mother and stayed hidden in the cave longer. If I had listened, I might be home with my dog Yo-na now."

Grandmother looked at the baby nestled in her new mother's arms. "That little one you're holding is glad you are here now, Grey Dove."

Grey Dove smiled down at the cooing baby. "Yes, she makes things better. I always wanted lots of children, but I lost my first one, a boy, in the early years of our marriage. Then I didn't get pregnant with Tsu-la until I was almost too old to have a baby." She stroked Tsu-la's gleaming black braids. "Her father and I were so happy when this one was born."

Tsu-la grinned at her mother and put her finger on the baby's nose. "And I am glad this one was born to be my sister."

GRANDMOTHER BEGAN SAVING her rations of bread so she could give them to Tsu-la when she came to see her each morning. The lively little girl chatted with Grandmother and begged Blue to tell her "just one more story about Yo-na."

One morning Tsu-la didn't come.

Grandmother paced and wrung her hands. "Bluebird, go check on Tsu-la. Something might have happened to her. So many are getting sick."

Blue knew something was wrong when she walked over to the section of the stockade where Tsu-la and her family stayed. She heard a baby crying and Tsu-la saying, "Be quiet now, Sister. I am doing the best I can. You can have all my bread. Just quit crying."

Tsu-la was huddled in a corner, holding her sister, attempting to feed the baby small pieces of torn-up bread. Blue put her hand on the little girl's shoulder. "Tsu-la, the bread must be soaked in milk before she can eat it."

Tsu-la raised her dirty, tear-stained face and looked at Blue. "I know, but I don't have any milk to soak it in. Mother always got the milk from the cook and soaked the bread."

Blue put her arm around the poor, trembling child. "Where is your mother?"

"The soldiers took her away last night."

"Where did they take her?"

"I don't know. They just picked her up and carried her away. I tried to talk to her, but she didn't say anything."

Blue offered her hand to Tsu-la and took the crying baby from her arms. "Let's go find some milk for your sister. You can stay with Grandmother and me for a while."

When Blue brought the children back to where Grandmother and Grey stayed, Grey greeted them with his usual scowl. "Why are you bringing them here? We don't have any extra food. They should be with their family."

Grandmother scolded him. "Tsu-la and A-wi-a-gi-na are our friends. We share what we have with our friends."

Blue nodded her head. "Yes, they are welcome to stay with us. After they eat, I will go see what I can find out about their family."

Later that night, after she had washed them off and settled the children in for the night, Blue motioned for Grandmother and Grey to join her outside their sleeping area. "I spoke to the people who slept close to Grey Dove. They said she died of a fever last night, and the soldiers removed her body this morning."

Grey sighed. "I am sorry for the little ones, but why didn't one of those people take them in?"

"They were afraid of the fever."

"Then perhaps we should also be afraid."

Grandmother snorted. "I am not afraid, and if I am not, neither should a strong young man be afraid. The children are healthy, and they need someone to take care of them. That's what we will do until they no longer need us."

"All right, but do you mind if I ask around to see if there is anyone else who might be better suited to take care of them?"

"I don't care. Go ahead and ask."

Grey came back an hour later with a middle-aged couple. They introduced themselves as Robert and Myrtle Wildcat. The husband was solemn and quiet, but his bubbly, mixed blood wife talked freely. "Robert and I have never had an easy life. My white father disowned me when I told him I wanted to marry a full blood and threatened to kill Robert, so we had to move far away. I lost a baby when we were first married, and I was never able to conceive another. Now we find ourselves here. But we would be happy if you would let us take care of these little girls, and we would do our best to keep them safe and loved."

Grandmother walked over to where the couple was standing and peered into their faces. "You look like good people, but these are special children. Tsu-la especially has been blessed by the Creator with intelligence and sensitivity. And these are hard times to raise a child in. Are you sure that you want to take them on?"

The husband cleared his throat and spoke in a quiet solemn voice. "All I can say is we want them, and we promise to do our best to protect them and provide for them."

Grey nodded. "They would be in good hands with the Wildcats."

"You are probably right, Grandson, but I want Tsu-la to meet them first. Can you come back in the morning?"

Mrs. Wildcat took Grandmother's hand. "Wa-do. We will be here after breakfast in the morning."

As Blue was brushing out Tsu-la's tangled locks, she tried to prepare her. "Tsu-la, you know your mother isn't coming back."

The little girl's lip quivered. "Yes, I know she is with the Creator. Back home Mother told me I had a big brother who died and is already with the Creator. Do you think they are together?"

"I am sure they are."

Tsu-la finally gave in to crying. Between sobs, she got out, "But I want my mother to be here with my sister and me."

"I know you do, but you know she can't come back to Earth even if she wants to."

Tsu-la dropped her eyes and sighed. "I know."

"I need to tell you something."

"What?"

"Someone is coming to meet you today. Their little baby left them to live with the Creator long ago, and they have been lonely. They want you and your sister to come live with them."

Tsu-la frowned. "But we want to stay with you and Grandmother."

"Just meet them, and then you can decide where it is best for you and your sister to stay. If you decide to stay here, you may."

"All right."

Blue had just finished feeding the baby when the Wildcats came to where she and Grandmother were sitting. Myrtle gushed over the baby. "What a pretty little doll! May I hold her?"

"Sure." Blue handed little A-wi-a-gi-na to Myrtle, and the baby grinned and settled comfortably in her arms.

Tsu-la stood back and watched the woman cuddle with her sister. Robert approached her with his hand outstretched. "Here, Tsu-la, I thought you might like some extra bread to eat."

Tsu-la grinned big and showed her missing front teeth. "Wa-do."

He smiled as he watched her eat. "Tsu-la, we would be very happy if you and your sister would come and live with us. "

Tsu-la brushed off her mouth and hands. "All right."

Then she ran over and hugged Grandmother, who kissed her cheek. "Come back and see me soon, Tsu-la."

Myrtle beamed. "She can come any time she wants to. Thank you for trusting us with these precious children."

Blue spoke up. "Don't forget to come see us, Tsu-la. I need someone I can tell stories to."

Tsu-la ran and hugged Blue. "I won't forget."

Blue had been so busy with the children she forgot about contacting her uncle. The next morning, the soldiers opened the stockade gates and drove the Cherokees out before them. When Blue realized they were finally leaving this place, she was almost happy. At least she would get some fresh air and get away from the stench of sickness and unsanitary living conditions. While she was in the stockade, she had seen several people sicken and die from high fevers or dysentery. There were days the collection wagons, which the soldiers brought into the stockade each day, were piled high with Cherokee bodies of all sizes and ages. There were nights when she couldn't sleep for the sounds of the crying and wailing that accompanied each new death.

THE FIRST DAYS of the long march were very hot for early summer, but far worse was the wear and tear of the long miles that had to be covered every day, all day, until evening time, which brought a chronic weariness to the bones. Even though Grandmother was allowed to ride in one of the slow-moving wagons, which carried the elderly, the disabled, the pregnant women, and small children, her body showed the strain of the hard journey. By the end of the first month, she was smaller and weaker than when Blue first met her.

Grandmother offered Blue a tin bowl that was nearly full. "Bluebird, would you like the rest of my stew? I have eaten all I can hold."

"Grandmother, you eat less each day. No, you eat it."

"Truly, child, I am not hungry, but I don't want to waste good food. How about you, Grey Wolf? Boys are always hungry."

"Only because you won't eat it. In a few days, the soldiers told us we could run ahead and try to snare some rabbits. Maybe you will eat more if we have fresh meat to put in the stew." Grey Wolf hastily gulped the remainder of the bowl down.

"Maybe so. Now, Grey, I know you. Don't you be trying to slip away when you are out hunting. It will just get you into trouble."

"I would like to, but I can't leave without you and Blue. You need me to take care of you."

Blue laughed. "You don't have to take care of me, boy. I take care of myself."

"I watch out for you more than you know, little girl."

Blue considered. Grey Wolf did have a way of turning up just when she was thinking of trying to run away.

Once when he saw her stop walking and look into the nearby woods, he said, "Not yet, Blue. The soldiers are watching you."

Blue looked at his scowling dark face, shrugged her shoulders, and kept walking.

The next morning Grandmother asked the soldiers if Bluebird

could ride in the wagon with her. "I am not well and need my granddaughter to take care of me."

"All right, but only until you get to feeling better. We need the young ones to walk 'cause these wagons are gettin mighty crowded."

What was Grandmother up to? Even though she was losing weight, she was still able to move about and take care of herself. She soon discovered Grandmother just wanted to talk. Endless stories of family history poured out, and Blue hungrily drank them all in.

Grandmother started one story with a question. "Do you know why your clan, the Bird clan, is important?"

"No. I am ashamed to say I know little about my clan."

"Don't be ashamed. I will tell you. The people of the Bird clan are messengers. Your people tell the Cherokees what is going on and warn them of danger. Because of them and their work, many Cherokees are alive today."

"How about the Wolf clan?"

"We are the warriors and the protectors of our people." Grandmother gave Blue a big smile, her dark eyes dancing, as if she hid a happy secret. "Do you know why I am telling you all of this?"

"I guess because you know I like to listen."

Grandmother's eyes danced some more. "That's part of it, but that's not the main reason. I think of you as my granddaughter, and I want to pass my family memories and stories on to you."

"Thank you, Grandmother, but why don't you tell Grey your stories? He's your grandson."

"For one thing, he isn't interested in my stories, and for another, that is not the way it is done in my family. In our family, the women are the ones who keep the stories and pass them down to our daughters and granddaughters. I think of you as a woman of my family."

"That is an honor, Grandmother. Tell me all of the stories you want. I will tell my daughter the stories of the Wolf clan someday."

"Yes, I know you will. Now I will tell you my secret, and why I am happy." Grandmother paused. "Someday this trail will end, and someday you will be part of the Wolf family."

"But I will always be a member of the Bird clan."

"I know that, but you can still be part of my family."

"How can that be?"

"Someday you and Grey Wolf will marry, and your children will be my great-grandchildren."

"I don't know about that, Grandmother. He called me 'Frog' yesterday because he said that I have big eyes and long skinny legs. I don't think Grey Wolf even likes me."

"And you don't know much about men, girl."

Lively Tsu-la also helped break up the monotony of life on the trail. Even though she was barely seven, the sturdy little girl walked beside her new father every day. Some days her mother would accompany them with her little sister on her hip. On those days, Blue noticed Robert slipping into the woods. He would catch up to the group a few minutes later with extra food for his family. If there was extra, Tsu-la brought a present to Grandmother, glowing with pride, as she gave her tiny bird eggs or a few handfuls of mushrooms or other edible plants, wrapped up in a clean cloth. If Grandmother claimed she wasn't hungry, Tsu-la, standing in front of her, with arms akimbo, would say, "I brought it to you, Granny, and I want to see you eat it."

Grandmother would say, "All right, stubborn child, I will eat, but can I give a little to Bluebird and Grey?"

"Just a little."

After the food was gone, Tsu-la would crawl into Blue's lap and demand a Yo-na story. Then Grey would say, "It's time to go back to your folks," and he would take Tsu-la's hand and escort her back to where her parents stayed with her baby sister.

From the wagon where she sat, Grandmother smiled as she watched Tsu-la walking beside her father each day. She made remarks about what Tsu-la was doing. "Look, Bluebird, she's found some pretty flowers today." On another day she said, "Her father is carrying her because she just stepped on a thorn."

Watching Tsu-la and telling Blue all kinds of family and Cherokee stories occupied most of Grandmother's time, and she seemed content.

That night Blue thought of all she had learned from Grandmother. Her mother wasn't much of a talker and didn't divulge much of their family's past. Blue, however, had a burning curiosity to learn everything and could sometimes pester a fact or story from her mother.

I should have asked her more questions and got her to talk more. Now it's too late, and I will never know. Grandmother is so wise, and I believe everything she has told me, except for the part about Grey and me getting married. It might be nice, though, to be part of the Wolf family.

Even though the next few days remained equally hot and dry, Grandmother's spirits stayed high. Her body might be frail, but her mind was still agile, which one soldier ruefully discovered. He was the soldier the girls called 'Spider' because like a spider's legs, his hands were constantly in motion, trying to feel or pinch the breasts or buttocks of girls and young women. Grandmother warned the girls to stay as far away from Spider as they could and to never go anywhere by themselves. She also kept her eyes trained on him so she could warn any female he was near.

One night, Little Deer, who was only a few months older than Blue, got up from the fire to relieve herself in the nearby woods. When she didn't come back, Grandmother arose, shook Grey and Blue awake and said, "Come, and bring your blankets."

She awoke some other women that slept nearby. "Bring what I told you to bring."

They followed Grandmother to hide in the bushes, behind a wagon where Spider, who was on guard duty, had Little Deer pinned. Speaking in Cherokee, Grandmother said, "Blankets!"

The biggest women jumped on Spider's back and held him to the ground while others swaddled him so tightly in blankets he couldn't move. Meanwhile Grandmother signaled for Blue to pull Little Deer loose, handed Grey cloth to blindfold the soldier, and signaled for him to assist with holding Spider down.

She and others chanted in English, "Pinch the spider!" Women, carrying buckets of crayfish, carefully put them down the soldier's shirt and pants. He began thrashing about and screaming in pain.

Grandmother yelled, "Run!" And they all sprang away from him and scattered to their sleeping spots seconds before the other soldiers awoke and came to see what was happening.

The girls and women tittered as the Lieutenant came upon Spider struggling to free himself from the blankets and pinching crayfish. After signaling for some nearby soldiers to assist Spider, the Lieutenant berated him. "My God, man! How did you let this happen to you?"

In the following weeks, Spider kept his hands to himself, but he took every opportunity to treat Grandmother and the other elders roughly. Once when Grey saw a black bruise on Grandmother's arm, he said, "I will kill the man who did this to you!"

Blue put her hand on his arm, but Grey shook it off. "Please, Grey. They will kill you."

Angry little Grandmother stared at Grey until he dropped his eyes. "Grey won't kill anyone because no one hurt me. I am getting old and clumsy, and I bruise at every little hurt I sustain."

"I don't believe you."

Grandmother grabbed Grey by the ear. "Are you calling your grandmother a liar?"

Grey's eyes grew huge with shock. "No, Grandmother. Why are you hurting me? You have never done anything to hurt me before."

Grandmother released his ear. "I had to be harsh so you would listen to me. Now do what your parents and grandfather would have wanted. Stay close to me and to Bluebird and don't throw your life away."

"All right, Grandmother. I will listen—for now."

Tsu-la brought Spider's wrath down on Grandmother. She was sitting in the wagon, watching Tsu-la as always, when Grandmother noticed a rattlesnake was coiled up a few feet in front of the child. She yelled out, "Tsu-la, stop, there is a snake close by!"

Robert grabbed the child and gave her into the care of a woman who was walking nearby. He picked up a large rock, walked over to the bush where the snake was coiled, and brought the rock down, smashing the snake's head. He yelled out, "Wa-do, Grandmother," and ran back to pick up Tsu-la.

Spider, who was riding close by, came up beside their wagon. "Any old lady who can yell like that don't need to be ridin in a wagon, and why are you still here, girl? You was just supposed to ride in here a day or two until your granny got to feelin better. Both of ya'll will be walkin after the noon meal."

When Blue told Grey what Spider said, he exploded. "That Spider has no right to make you walk! No other grandmother has to walk, and neither should you!"

"I have no choice."

Grey's grim smile chilled Blue's blood. "But I have a choice, and I choose to stomp an ugly Spider."

Again, Blue laid her hand on Grey's arm. "No, Grey. Let me talk to the Lieutenant. He will tell Spider Grandmother can ride in the wagon. For myself, I don't mind walking."

"Let her talk to him, Grey."

"All right, but if he says no, I will talk to that Spider myself."

Blue ran through the camp, seeking the Lieutenant. She ran up to the man the Lieutenant called Lucas. "Where is the Lieutenant?"

He glared at her over his cup of coffee. "Don't you know better than to bother folks when they're eatin? The lieutenant ain't here. He rode ahead to scout out the trail. Go on back where you belong."

Blue knew it would do no good, but she said, "Please, sir."

"I ain't got time for your little problems. Go on back now, gal, before you make me mad."

Blue walked back slowly, trying to come up with a plan. When she got back, Grey was handing their metal dishware back to the cooks for cleaning. "Well, what did he say?"

"Nothing. He's not here."

"Well, I will pay a visit to the Spider."

Grandmother stood up and faced him. "But I want to walk. I am eating more, and I feel strong. I will walk. If little Tsu-la can walk, so can I."

Grey stared at her. "Are you sure?"

"Yes. I will walk close to Blue. I can lean on her if I get tired."

"All right then, but I have my eye on you."

Grandmother kept up fine for the first hour. Tsu-la noticed her presence and ran back to show her a butterfly she had caught. "See what I have found, Granny. Are you going to walk with us now?"

"Oh, that's a pretty one. Be careful you don't crush it. Yes, I will be walking with you now."

"Good! And I know not to hurt things. See, I'm letting her fly off my finger. See you later, Granny." She ran off to rejoin her father.

Grandmother began lagging behind, and she motioned to Blue for help. Blue supported her weight, and they struggled along for another half hour or so. Grey and his friend Strong Bear came back to where they were. Strong Bear lowered himself on his big haunches. "Climb on my back, Grandmother. I will carry you."

"No, I am too heavy for you to carry so far."

Grey laughed. "Granny, on Strong Bear's broad back, you will look like a horsefly on a big horse."

"All right then. We can try it."

Blue helped position her. "Put your arms around his neck."

"Here we go, but don't let me choke you, boy."

"What did you say, horsefly? When are you going to get on my back, Grandmother?"

Granny laughed and gently tugged Strong Bear's ear. "Be careful, horse. The fly might bite you."

Blue breathed a sigh of relief as Strong Bear, Grey, and Grandmother continued to tease and laugh at each other. Once Grey threw up his hand to stop Strong Bear. "You have been carrying her for over three hours, it's time I take a turn."

"If you want, but I'm not tired at all."

Granny spoke up. "But it is hot, and you need to stop and get cooled down."

"That's true. I could use a drink."

Blue gave him a dipperful from the bucket she was carrying. He took a big gulp and splashed the rest on his face. "Wa-do, Blue. The water is good and cold."

"Raven and her sisters ran ahead and found a cold spring. They have been giving buckets of water to everyone."

Strong Bear's grin reached from ear to ear, and his voice sounded warm and honeyed. "Raven is a good woman."

Grey jostled Granny as he leaned a bit to poke Strong Bear in the side. "Says the man who loves her."

Granny hissed. "Careful! My last horse was a much smoother ride."

They all laughed, and the miles and the day soon ended. The next day the young men continued to take turns carrying Granny. Tsu-la came by once and said, "I want a ride."

Grey shuddered in mock fright. "I don't know if this horse is strong enough to carry such a big girl."

Tsu-la punched him in the arm. "I'm not that big!"

"Ouch! All right then. Climb on up."

She giggled and stayed on Grey's back until the noon meal when she rejoined her family. After eating, she resumed walking beside her father.

EARLY THE NEXT morning, the Lieutenant rode by on his big sorrel. He suddenly whirled around and came back to where they were walking. "What are you doing carrying an older person on your back? Anyone unable to walk is supposed to ride in a wagon."

Grey motioned for Blue to speak. "A soldier told our grandmother she would have to walk. When she couldn't, her grandson and his friend started carrying her."

The Lieutenant frowned. "Which soldier told her that?"

Blue pointed to Spider, who was casting furtive glances in their direction. "That one."

"I will speak to him directly. Help your grandmother mount my horse, and I will return her to where she needs to be."

"Thank you, Lieutenant."

"You're welcome."

It wasn't long before Blue noticed Spider was now assigned to helping the main cook prepare food. Grey walked by and smirked at him every chance he got.

As time went on, there were more and more days when all Grandmother wanted to do was rest and read the brown book she kept by her side. One day, after the midday meal was finished, Raven, her sister Mockingbird, and four other young women approached Blue.

Raven asked, "Would you like to take a bath in the creek with us? The soldiers said we are going to camp here for a while so that they can make some wagon repairs."

Bird looked at Grandmother for an answer.

"Go ahead and have some fun, girl. You don't have to sit by my side every minute. I am just going to rest and read today. Here, better take an extra blanket to wrap up in. You don't want to catch a chill."

SOON THE GIRLS were laughing and splashing each other. Even though the water was freezing because it was fed by a spring, it felt good to wash the dirt of the journey from their skins. For a few minutes, Blue could splash in the water and pretend she was just having fun with some friends, instead of being on a forced march. Finally, the girls climbed out of the cold water and sat around a small fire that they had built to keep warm while their clothes dried on some nearby bushes.

The oldest girl, Katie Springwater, cut her eyes over at Blue. "Are you in love with Grey Wolf?"

"No, of course not. I'm not in love with anybody."

Running Squirrel huffed and smirked. "Why did you ask her that? Can't you see she is just a little girl? That wolf is not a cub anymore. He's almost a full-grown man. Bluebird wouldn't know what to do with a man. Now I, I would know what to do with him."

"So would I," said Tall Girl, Strong Bear's sister. "If he would give me a chance."

Now it was Blue's turn to smirk. "He won't. Grey Wolf doesn't like girls."

Raven's sister, Mockingbird, laughed. "That's the point, little girl. He might not like girls, but I bet he would like women."

Running Squirrel chimed in. "They're right, Bluebird. Little girls like you are flat as boards, all arms and legs. Grey Wolf likes women who look like me." At this the girl dropped her blanket and showed off her full body.

"Ha! Is that all you have to share? Look at these!" The buxom girl named Bright Turtle dropped her blanket to the ground.

All of the girls giggled, except for Bluebird and Raven. Raven wagged her finger at them, scolding. "Stop being foolish, girls! Someone might see. Now put your blankets back on."

Blue started at the sound of a twig breaking. "What was that?"

Raven jumped to her feet. "Someone has been watching us! Quick, wrap back up and grab your clothes. We need to get back to camp."

Before they could leave, two laughing young soldiers came through the bushes where they had been hiding. The taller of the two swigged something from a jug but put it down when his short, stocky friend spoke.

"What's your hurry, girls? We was enjoyin' the show. "

Their blue eyes glazed with drink and lust, the soldiers swaggered toward the girls. The tall, thin one spoke as he removed his gun belt. "Don't run away, girlies. We just want to have a little fun with you. It won't hurt much."

Raven screamed, "Run! Leave your clothes!"

The short one grabbed her, and she fought to get out of his grasp.

Blue was the first back to camp, screaming as she ran. "The soldiers have Raven! They are going to hurt her!"

Grey Wolf asked, "Where is she?"

"By the creek. We were bathing. Hurry, Grey, get your friends and go save her!"

"Those dirty soldiers are going to get what's coming to them!" He ran off, shouting for his friends to come to him.

By this time, the other girls had arrived. Katie ran up to her father and begged, "Please, Father, help Raven get away from the soldiers."

"I want to, Daughter, but this is soldier business. They will shoot us if we go alone. Bluebird, run and get the Lieutenant. You other girls, get back to the wagons."

"Grey Wolf is on his way to find his friends and rescue Raven."

"We'll try to head them off. Now, run, Bluebird!"

The Lieutenant hurried from where he was camped with his men when he heard his name called.

"Lieutenant, please come. Your soldiers are hurting girls."

"What's that? Take me where this is happening. Joe, Dan, and Lucas, come with me."

By the time they arrived at the spot, some of the elders had pulled the soldiers off of Raven and were restraining them. The younger men, including Grey, were being kept away by the older men. But Blue could hear them murmuring angrily in Cherokee.

"Thank you for helping, men, but we'll take care of this situation now. You can all leave."

The Lieutenant took off his jacket and covered Raven's nakedness. "Little girl, you can take your friend back to camp. Thanks for coming to get me."

Grey stepped forward to help Blue get Raven to her feet. He scowled at the cowering soldiers when he saw her battered bloody face.

The Cherokees' medicine man, Running Deer, gently moved Grey aside and took his place at Raven's side. "Go on back to camp, Grey Wolf. You don't need to be here. Little Bluebird and I will take Raven back to the wagon where my wife and I will doctor her. Then she will go back to her family."

Grey and his friends stalked away, still murmuring in Cherokee.

LATER, BLUE HEARD Raven and her sisters crying throughout the night. Once Grandmother sighed and left the place where she was sleeping. She walked to a place in the shadows and knelt. She prayed for a few minutes and came back to her spot between Blue and Grey. Blue nestled closer to Grandmother and resolved never to leave her side again.

"Will she be all right, Grandmother?"

"She will, in time. She's just frightened. Big Bear told me the Lieutenant got there in time to keep those bad soldiers from finishing what they had started with her. He told them they were no longer wanted in his service, so you don't have to worry about them anymore. He took away all their soldier gear, gave them some food, and told them they can walk back to the nearest town. Still, it's better if you girls stay close to the wagons in the future. We don't want any other girl getting hurt. Now go to sleep."

But Grey had overheard them speaking, and his words escaped in a torrent. "She's more than frightened, Grandmother. You should have seen her face! It was covered with blood where those dog soldiers hit her when she was fighting back. If the old men hadn't stopped us, we would have killed those dogs who did that to her! But, no, we have to be cowards and let the whites hurt our women. It makes me sick!"

"Better sick than dead, boy. Now settle down and go to sleep. You have a hard day's walk ahead of you tomorrow."

"All right, Granny, but just so you know, I won't always be a coward. One day I will have my revenge on those dog soldiers."

The next day, after supper, Grey took Blue aside and whispered in her ear. "Walk down to the river with me."

BLUE LOOKED AROUND, checked that no one was watching them, and followed Grey's retreating figure. He stopped at the foot of a tall willow tree. "See this willow tree? It's the only one of its kind around here. Do you think you could find it again at twilight?"

Blue studied the tree. "I could find it, but why?"

"You'll understand later, I promise. Just bring Raven and meet me here at twilight."

"What if she won't come?"

"She'll come. "

"What if we're caught and get in trouble?"

"You won't be."

Blue shook her head. "It sounds like a bad idea. I don't want to chance it."

Grey took her by the shoulders and looked into her eyes. "Do you trust me, Blue?"

Blue stared into the grave dark eyes. "My heart trusts you, but my mind says not to."

"Listen to your heart."

"All right, but only if Raven agrees to come."

"She will come."

GREY NOTICED BLUE'S nervous fidgeting.

GRANDMOTHER NOTICED BLUE'S nervous fidgeting. "What's wrong?"

Blue took a deep breath. It was hard to lie to Grandmother. "I have been feeling queasy today. I think I will walk around the camp and get some fresh air."

"All right. Just don't get too far away. It would be wise to get another girl to walk with you."

"Good idea, Grandmother. I will see if Raven will walk with me."

"Just be back before dark."

"We will."

Blue walked over to where Raven's family slept. She smiled at Raven's mother. "I was looking for Raven."

Raven's mother's eyes were red, with dark circles under them, but she tried to return Blue's smile. "She is standing over with Bright Turtle."

Blue looked into Raven's dark haunted eyes. "Are you all right?"

"I am fine. Let's go. Bright Turtle is walking with us."

"You know what Grey said for us to do."

"Yes, we both know."

Bright Turtle took Blue's arm and started chatting about the different young men in the camp. When Blue didn't respond, she pinched her and whispered, "Quit looking so scared. We are three friends out for a walk."

Raven joined in, talking loudly in English. "I think Grey Wolf is better-looking than anyone. What do you think, Blue?"

Blue stuttered a bit but managed to get out, "Oh, I don't know. I haven't really thought about it."

As they approached the young soldier on guard duty, Bright Turtle giggled and spoke louder. "I don't agree. I prefer the handsome soldiers over our Indian boys. Good evening, soldier. What is your name?"

The soldier, who wasn't much older than Raven, grinned broadly and said, "Name's Josh Goodman. And who are you ladies?"

Bright Turtle left them and stood close to the young soldier. She placed her arm on his shoulder and turned him away from his view of the river. "I am Bright Turtle, and these are my friends, Raven and Bluebird. Sit down here beside me on this rock, and let's get acquainted. Go on, girls. I am going to be busy for a while."

AS THEY WERE walking away, Blue caught a glimpse of Grey stealing his way to the river. The soldier was too busy staring at Bright Turtle's big bosom to notice. Raven said, "Come on. He's not looking," and they followed in the same direction that Grey had taken.

They remained silent until Raven asked, "Do you know where the tree is?"

"I think so. I believe it's over that way. It's the only willow."

"I see it, and Grey is waiting for us."

Grey said, "See, Blue. There was nothing to worry about."

"We're not back yet."

"You worry too much."

RAVEN'S FACE DARKENED. "Quit playing! Where are they?"

"Here under the willow."

"Do you have proof?"

Grey opened his hand to show the two objects he held. "Yes, here is the watch which the tall man had in his pocket, and this pipe belonged to the short one."

"But I can't keep the watch or the pipe?"

"No, someone might see you with them and start asking questions. You can have this." He handed her a gold locket.

Raven caressed the necklace with her fingers. "I was wondering what happened to my locket." She opened the locket and took out two locks of hair, one blond and one reddish brown. Raven took a deep breath, slowly exhaled, and smiled. She placed the hair back in the locket, closed it, and put it back around her neck. "Wa-do, Grey Wolf."

"You're welcome. I told you I would have revenge on those dog soldiers. I had to have some help, and it took a little time, but it's done. Now you have revenge, too."

"Yes, I do, and now I can sleep again."

"You girls better go back and rescue Bright Turtle. She is probably getting tired of dodging that dog's paws."

When the girls got back, they were surprised to see that Bright Turtle and the soldier were gone. A different young soldier was on guard duty. Blue was shaking, but she made herself speak to him. "Where are Bright Turtle and the soldier who was here before you?"

He ignored her question. "Where have you girls been? You should be with your families, gettin ready to turn in."

Raven spoke up. "I am sorry. I was helping my young friend with women matters."

The soldier turned bright red. He finally stammered a few words. "Guess that's all right. Just get to where you need to be."

As they walked away, Blue whispered, "But, Raven... what about Bright Turtle?"

"I will have to tell her father we don't know where she is. He will find her then."

As the girls turned the corner, they heard a familiar giggle. Bright Turtle, naked from the waist up, was sitting under a tree between Goodman and another soldier. The men were openly fondling her, and all three were taking turns swigging from a whiskey bottle. Raven stopped and held out her hand to the drunken girl. "Bright Turtle, come with us. Your family will be worried about you."

Bright Turtle just waved at them and spoke in slurred English. "No, go on without me, I have new friends, and we are having fun."

Goodman put out his hand and made a grab at Raven but missed. "Come on, pretty squaw. We got room for you too."

Raven took a step backward. She gritted her teeth and glared at Bright Turtle. "You will be sorry when I tell your father."

Bright Turtle staggered to an upright position and waved her arms. "Go away and leave me alone."

Then she collapsed, vomited all over herself, and passed out. The two men looked at her in disgust, picked up the nearly empty jug and left her lying in the dirt. Raven sighed and asked Blue to help get their friend on her feet. Bright Turtle's father came upon them as they were attempting to clean off the vomit and straighten her clothes. "What happened to her?"

Raven shifted Bright Turtle's body to her father's arm. "She can tell you after she comes to herself. We need to go to our families."

As they walked away, Blue whispered a question. "Why didn't you tell him she got drunk with the soldiers?"

"Bright Turtle got in trouble trying to help me, and she is my friend. It's her decision what she wants to tell her father. I just hope it doesn't happen again."

During the following weeks, many of the soldiers laughed whenever they saw Bright Turtle. If no officers were around, they made lewd gestures and directed obscene remarks to her. Bright Turtle cried and ran away each time it happened. The first time it happened her father shook his fist at the soldiers. He was thrown to the ground, kicked, and beaten. The next time it happened he turned his head and stared into space.

It wasn't long before the effects of Bright Turtle's depression manifested in her body. Seemingly overnight the once buxom, plump young woman transformed into a thin wraith who never spoke or showed emotion. Blue couldn't stand watching Bright Turtle suffer anymore. She went to Grandmother for advice. "Grandmother, how can I help Bright Turtle?"

Grandmother paused in brushing her long silver hair. "It is her family's place to help her."

"Her mother died in the stockade. Her father is old and can't stand any more beatings."

"Then her clan should help her."

"Who is in her clan?"

"She belongs to the Deer clan. I will speak to the clan women and see if we can get her some help."

Blue gently took the brush from Grandmother's hand. "Here, let me. You missed a spot."

As she brushed the silver hair, she smiled. "Thank you, Grandmother. Now everything will be all right."

Grandmother's dancing eyes turned dull and sad. "No, Bluebird. Everything will never be all right again, but we will do what we can to make it tolerable for the present."

THAT EVENING GRANDMOTHER ate with the Deer clan. After supper, she stayed and talked with the women of the clan. When she came back at bedtime, she whispered to Blue. "It's done."

"What has been done?"

"Bright Turtle is now Crawling Snake's woman."

Blue shuddered as she thought of the once carefree girl, lying with the grim-faced, middle-aged Cherokee man. "But Crawling Snake never smiles, and he is twice her age. The younger men all say they are afraid of him because one misspoke word earns them a slap. Only Grey and Strong Bear aren't afraid of him."

"Yes, I know. Grey wants to attack the soldiers when they torment Bright Turtle, but I have asked Strong Bear to restrain him every time he starts moving toward them. I need to tell you something. Crawling Snake used to smile before his wife and children died of dysentery in the stockade. Such hardships make a man bitter and hard. Even the soldiers fear him, and that is what Bright Turtle needs, a strong man to protect her."

Soon Bright Turtle was never seen without Crawling Snake. If a soldier even looked at her, Crawling Snake's malevolent gaze would make them drop their eyes. As for Bright Turtle, she never regained her sunny disposition or plump figure, but she stopped staring into space and even managed a slight smile now and then. Crawling Snake never showed Bright Turtle affection, but Blue noticed a different look in his eyes when he looked at his young wife. It was a soft look no one else received from the stern man.

Blue burned with curiosity to know how Grey managed to kill Raven's attackers. One night after Grandmother started to snore, Blue moved over to Grey's side.

"How did you kill those men?"

"Wait until this trail ends, and I will tell you."

Blue spent some time awake, wondering what other secrets Grey kept from her.

THE DAYS DRAGGED on, each morning bringing even hotter, drier conditions than before. Blue heard the soldiers speaking about a drought. Grey and the other young men watched the soldiers with eyes full of hate, and the Lieutenant seemed to know it. He made a great show of talking roughly to his soldiers about the two who had attempted the rape. If he was rough with his soldiers, he was the opposite to the Cherokees, speaking quietly and offering them extra food and blankets.

"You folks could use some good meat. Why don't your young men run ahead of the company and hunt for your people? The cook will give you some rope, knives, and other materials to make traps with."

Grey Wolf spat as a soldier extended his hand. The soldier pulled back and frowned, but at the Lieutenant's nod, reached out once again. Grey Wolf's dark eyes turned black, but he took the offered knife from the soldier's hand. Bird watched him, knowing how much he wanted to use the knife on the soldier.

That evening Grey Wolf and some younger men and boys brought several rabbits to the campfire, much to the delight of one of the Cherokee women who sometimes helped with the cooking. "Thank you, men. We will have good meat for our stew in the morning. Come on, women, let's skin the tsi-s-du the young men have brought us. A rich stew will make us a fine meal."

The women took turns keeping the big pots cooking most of the night. In the morning, everyone was happy to devour the good, hot stew, all except Grandmother. She ate a few bites and gave the rest to Grey Wolf, even though he scolded her for not eating.

TIME PASSED SO slowly, and it seemed like they had been traveling for years, instead of weeks. One day a dry, howling wind entered the camp, sucking away the energy and the lives of the Cherokees. Blue knew something was different when she couldn't rouse Grandmother that morning. "Wake up, Grandmother. It's time to get up."

Grandmother just moaned and fell back to sleep.

Blue reached across Grandmother's body to touch Grey Wolf's shoulder. "Grey, I can't wake Grandmother up!"

"What? Let me try."

Grey Wolf gently shook his grandmother. "Granny, wake up!"

The only response was a low moan.

Grey touched Grandmother's forehead. "Blue, she's burning up. Go, get the healer."

The medicine man, Running Deer, seemed to have aged several

years since Blue had seen him last. His hair had grown white, and his body was stooped.

"I will come with you, Bluebird, but there may be nothing I can do. So many have died, and I couldn't save them. I couldn't even save my own wife, but I will come." He brushed his hand across his eyes and picked up his medicine bag.

Running Deer shook his head when he looked at Grandmother. "There's nothing I can do for her and the others except say their burial prayers. Her spirit has almost left her body. Stay close to her and keep her warm. I am sorry, children."

He patted Grey's shoulder and walked away. Grey struggled to maintain his composure.

Blue didn't try to stop her emotions. She wailed and cried out. "You can't leave us, Grandmother. We need you."

Grey grabbed her in a rough embrace. "It's no use, Blue. She is going to be with our people who have passed over. My mother is waiting for her."

"What will I do without her, Grey? I lost my mother, my home, and now I am losing Grandmother."

"It's all right, Blue. You still have me, and now we can run away from these whites and go back home."

Blue looked into his dark eyes and felt his thick black hair cascade around her shoulders. He drew her close, and she felt his strength. Grey brought a sense of security and comfort to Bird's heavy heart.

Yes, together they could find their way back home. It was just a matter of time.

The two youngsters spent that day with their arms around their grandmother, nestling close to the woman they both loved. So many people had fallen sick that the Lieutenant allowed the company to halt for one day. The able-bodied men were put to work digging graves because it was apparent that several were very ill, and some were on the brink of death.

Sometime during the long day, Blue dozed off. She awakened when she felt Grey's hand on her shoulder.

"She's gone, Blue. I'll go make sure there is a grave ready for her, and I will tell the women to come help you with her body."

When Grey left her side, Blue wiped her tears and gently closed Grandmother's eyes. "Goodbye, Grandmother. I will always love and remember you. "

She kissed the dear little face and gathered clean rags and water. She was soon joined by some of the other Cherokee women who instructed her on how to prepare a body for burial.

The Lieutenant agreed to delay their departure a few hours the next morning to allow the Cherokees to say goodbye to Grandmother and four more elders who had died that night. Big Bear quickly fashioned five crosses from some boards the cook had given him.

Blue watched him as Bear fashioned several more crosses. "Why did you make those? We are only burying five."

He smiled kindly at her. "Because I have a feeling that these will not be the only graves we dig. Yes, these twelve will be needed and several more."

Big Bear's prediction proved itself early the next morning. Little Tsu-la came running to Blue, crying, saying, "Where is Grandmother? I need to talk to her."

Blue grabbed the little girl and held her close. "Grandmother is in the spirit world now."

Tsu-la cried and sobbed even harder. "So is Sister."

"Oh, no, Tsu-la! I am so sorry."

Grey returned to find the two girls, holding each other, and rocking back and forth in their grief. He put his arms around both of them, and the three children grieved together.

At the joint service, one of the older men, Spotted Horse, had a Cherokee Bible from which he read a few verses. Blue was surprised to hear Grey Wolf quote the scriptures, word for word, along with the elder. Blue looked around and saw Tsu-la's adoptive parents, sitting with their arms around Tsu-la. They looked shocked and lost. Everywhere she looked she saw pain and despair. Then the Hummingbird family began singing "One Drop of Blood." The beautiful song touched her heart and the souls of the sad Cherokees around her, and she joined in with the others as they sang together.

Since it was necessary to have six funerals at once, attendees visited each newly dug grave and threw a handful of soil in with the tightly bound bodies. As they finished throwing in the soil for each grave, Running Deer recited a Cherokee burial prayer. The grave was filled in with dirt, and Big Bear placed one of his hand-made wooden crosses at its head. Grandmother was the last body buried. After everyone else had left, Grey and Bird lingered by the grave.

"Grey, I didn't know you followed the white man's religion."

"I don't, not really, but Granny always made me go to church with her, and she brought her Cherokee Bible with her. That's what you used to see her read sometimes."

"I always wondered what that book was. May I see it sometime?"

"Sure, but you can't read it, can you?"

"No, I just want to hold it. It will remind me of Grandmother. Grey, what kind of medicine did that song have?"

"I'm not sure, but I think it was the healing kind."

The Lieutenant called out. "Time to move out, folks! We need to get some miles in before dark."

Grey took her hand and helped her to her feet. "Guess we better join the others. Goodbye, Granny."

"Goodbye, Grandmother. We will miss you."

Each day grew hotter, and with the hotter weather came more disease, more deaths, and more tears. One morning Bird saw Big Bear gathering wood for more crosses.

He greeted her. "Si-yo. They should call this journey a trail of tears since there have been so many deaths and so many tears shed."

"Si-yo. Yes, they could call it that, all right. How many have there been now?"

"My last count showed fifteen, but I think there will be more. Remember, that's not counting all who have died on the other trips we don't know about. "

Bird thought about her mother and gave up all hope. Lame Bird could not have survived her own trail of tears.

The days grew unbearably hot, but the nights remained fairly cool while Bird watched Grey for a sign they were running away. Her eyes weren't the only ones on his broad-shouldered, narrow-hipped physique. Several girls looked at him, hoping to catch him looking back, but he never did.

ONE NIGHT, GREY Wolf woke Blue by putting his hand over her mouth.

He whispered, "It's time. Get your things."

Blue had been expecting his summons. She snatched the soft deerskin bag she had been carrying and quickly rolled it into her blankets. Then she put on her shoes and shawl. Noiselessly, she and Grey stole away from camp to a thicket where he had hidden two horses.

"I never asked you, but I suppose you can ride a horse?"

"Of course. We once had one, but she got old and died."

"Well, the horse I stole for you isn't an old nag."

"I will be fine. Let's go."

"Not too fast at first, Blue. We can't build up any speed until we are out of earshot."

Blue sighed. "I know. Now quit talking to me so we can get away."

They picked their way out of the woods until they came to a clearing. "Now, run, Blue. Run to freedom!"

Blue let her horse have his head, and he took off in a fast gallop. *He is strong! I hope I can handle him.*

She kept up with Grey Wolf until they came to a stream of water.

Grey cursed. "The water is too deep here. We must be getting close to that other big river the whites say we must cross on flat boats like we did before. Now we will have to waste time looking for a way to ford it. Better follow it upstream and look for a place to cross. At least the moon has come out, so we can see our way better."

"But that means that the soldiers will soon see that we are gone."

"I know, but we still have a chance. We just got to find a place to cross in a hurry."

A few minutes later Grey called out, "I think I found a place. You go on ahead of me so I can watch you. Careful now."

Blue tentatively urged her horse into the cold water. He immediately balked and stopped.

"Come on, Blue, kick him in the flanks and make him go!"

Blue kicked, and the horse waded into water, nickering nervously. Grey followed her.

Blue's feet dangled into the chilly water. "The river's getting deeper. "It's almost to his belly."

"Keep on going. You're halfway across."

Suddenly Blue's horse stumbled, reared, and threw her off. The shock of the fall and the ice-cold water prevented her from coming to the surface for a few seconds. Her mouth and nose filled with water, and she finally came up sputtering. Her horse swam the rest of the way across and took off in a run.

Grey Wolf saw what happened and called out, "Are you all right? Can you swim across? I need to catch your horse. I'll catch him and meet you on the other side. He still has your bag and blankets tied to him."

"I'm all right. Go ahead and catch him."

When Blue finally made it to the other side, she didn't see Grey, but she knew he was somewhere close by. Hoof beats thundered in the distance. They were caught.

She tried to run, but one of the soldiers, an older bewhiskered man with sad eyes, dismounted, caught her, and held her fast in front of him. "No use strugglin, girl. We'll see what the Lieutenant wants to do with you and your friend. They'll catch him soon, and we'll take you both back to camp."

"Run, Grey!" she screamed in Cherokee, but she knew it was no use. Too many men rode after him. When they brought Grey back, he was tied behind one of their horses, struggling to keep up. His face was bloody, and he held his right hand over his rib cage. In his hand was her bag. When he tried to give it to her, one of the young soldiers clouted him on the ear.

"Hey now!" said her captor. "Leave off that beatin. The Lieutenant said not to hurt him. Here, give me the girl's bag." He handed the bag to Blue.

One of the young soldiers turned and spat a gob of tobacco on Grey's head. "Ah, you're soft, Charlie, and so's the Lieutenant. These dirty Injuns cost us two or three hours of good travel time. He deserved what he got."

Charlie looked down at the slender young girl who was shivering and sobbing in his arms. He pulled out a handkerchief, from his shirt pocket, in which he had wrapped a stick of peppermint candy. He unwrapped the candy, and offered it to Blue.

She looked into the old soldier's eyes and noticed his tears. Her stomach growled at the sight of food. Blue took the offering, sniffed it, and gave it a tentative lick.

"Thank you."

"What? You can talk English? "

"A little."

"Well, go ahead and eat it, but please don't look at me. I can't stand lookin at those Cherokee eyes of yours. I seen eyes just like them, starin at me from the trees when I had to capture their owners and put them in a dirty stockade. Then I saw some of them same eyes when all the light went out of them before they died. Lord, it's a sad business! Least you don't have hate in your eyes like your friend."

Blue bit into the candy, lowered her eyes, and began staring at the ground.

Charlie reached out a gnarled hand to gently stroke Blue's hair. "That's all right, little girl. You can look at my ugly old face all you want to. Don't make no difference no how. I'm goin to see Cherokee eyes in my dreams for the rest of my life I reckon."

Charlie wiped a tear from his eye, gave a small quick kick to his horse's flank, and galloped to rejoin the other riders.

WHEN THEY GOT back to camp, the Lieutenant ordered their hands bound. After the company completed crossing the river on flat boats that morning, they walked all the rest of the day, and Grey stumbled as he went. They were not given any food or water until the company camped for the night. After their evening meal, they were tied to two separate wagon wheels to prevent them from talking to each other. Blue's joints and bones ached from the pain of lying on the hard ground without any comfort except for a ragged, old blanket that had been thrown down for her to lie on. Blue finally cried for mercy when Big Bear, the cross maker, brought her an extra blanket late in the night.

"Please, Bear, please ask the Lieutenant to let Grey Wolf and me sleep around the fire with the others. The ground is so cold and hard tonight, and Grey has been coughing. Every time he coughs, he groans. I think his ribs are hurt."

"I already talked to him, Granddaughter. He said sleeping this way tonight will be your only punishment, but you both have to swear that you will never try to run away again."

"I will swear, but I don't know if Grey will."

"I think Grey Wolf will do anything that you ask him to do."

Grey didn't like it, but when Blue begged him to swear, he agreed. The rest of their long journey was not uneventful. Most of the elders died because their bodies weren't strong enough to withstand the hardships of the Trail. Dysentery and other diseases swept through the camp and killed many of the old and young. Some died from accidents which would have been treatable if they had happened in a cleaner environment. Running Squirrel's moccasins wore so thin she sustained a large cut on the bottom of her right foot. The cut became infected, the infection spread through her bloodstream, and the young woman soon died. By the end of the journey, Big Bear, the cross maker, was buried under one of the last crosses that he made.

Thirty-nine members of their company were gone by the time they reached the end of their trail of tears.

III

A NEW HOME

THE COMPANY WHICH finally arrived at Fort Gibson in Indian Territory bore little resemblance to the group that had left Georgia some four months before. The original group had been teeming with people of all ages, from infants to elders like Grandmother and Big Bear. The hard journey had almost completely decimated those two groups, and mostly what remained were thin, sad middle-aged folks and hard, bitter young men like Grey Wolf. The trail had especially been hard on females, and by its end, the surviving men greatly outnumbered the women. A few older children had survived and had been adopted by some of the married adults, but they appeared to be miniature versions of their adoptive parents, seeming to have forgotten how to play and laugh.

Tsu-la was the exception. Blue watched Tsu-la and her parents join a large group of Cherokees, who all bore a resemblance to Tsu-la's tall solemn father. Tsu-la ran to join a circle of new young cousins who were laughing and playing a game. They broke ranks to include Tsu-la in the circle, and in a few minutes, she was giggling as she chased a tall girl who looked to be about the same age.

"Tsu-la looks happy, but what should we do, Grey?"

"I don't know, just wait until we're told what to do, I suppose."

"That one woman outside the gate keeps staring at us. Do you know who she is?"

"I'm not sure, but she looks like my cousin's wife. I never talked to her much because she was mostly white. Grandmother told me some of our relatives came here on their own. We thought they were disloyal to Chief Ross, but maybe they were the smart ones. At least they didn't have to go through what we did."

The woman said something to the soldiers who were guarding them, and she was permitted to speak to them. Blue noticed her Cherokee was halting like she was trying to remember the words. "Hello, aren't you Grey Wolf? I believe you are a cousin of my husband. His name is Ben Wolf, and I am his wife, Molly. You have changed so much that I barely knew you."

"Yes, I am. And this is my friend, Bluebird. We came over the trail together."

In Cherokee, she said, "Please forgive me, but I have forgotten most of the Cherokee I once knew. Do you... understand English at all, Bluebird?"

Blue nodded and said, "Yes, I understand some."

"Well, please tell Grey Wolf the soldiers are allowing relatives to take in the people who just arrived. Would the two of you like to stay with Ben and me? We have a small farm on the outskirts of Tahlequah. We could use your help, and it looks like you could use some regular meals and a comfortable place to sleep."

Blue delivered the message to Grey. He nodded his head and smiled at Molly. Then he told Blue what to say.

"Yes, we would like that, just until we can get our own place. We are going to get married in a few years."

Blue gasped when she heard the word "married", and her mind required time to process her thoughts. *Grey has always treated me like his little sister, so I didn't think he would marry me, but of course, we will get married. He just never has asked me. There is no one I care to spend my life with but Grey. I will always be safe with him.*

When he saw she had stopped talking, Grey elbowed her in the ribs to keep her on task. Blue looked over at him, grinned broadly, and relayed his message.

WHEN BLUE AND Grey stepped onto the porch of the neat, well-built log house, Blue couldn't hide her excitement. "Molly, do we really get to stay in this pretty house?"

Before Molly could answer, Ben, a short, stocky Cherokee man, slapped Grey on the back and greeted them in Cherokee. "Si-yo, cousins. I am so glad you made it through the trail and are going to live with us."

Grey smiled. "Wa-do, cousin, for letting us stay. We will work hard to show you our appreciation."

Molly snorted. "I didn't understand a word you all said except Wa-do. Please remember to speak English in this house."

Grey's smile faded, but Blue replied in English. "We will try, Molly. I understand most English but can only speak some. Grey can speak very little."

Molly put her arms around Blue and gave her a quick hug. "Don't you worry, sweet girl. You'll both be talkin proper English in no time."

Ben and Molly were kind to Grey and Blue, and Blue grew to appreciate Molly for her patience and determination to teach her new cousin how to properly keep house and manage a household. "No, Bluebird, you are overworkin the pie dough again. Remember good dough is made with gentle hands. Now let's start over."

And Blue would start over once again and never complain. She wanted to learn how to be a good housewife so she would be ready when she and Grey married. If only Grey were as compliant! Sometimes Blue wondered if the roomy log house was large enough to contain the four of them when Ben and Grey began to argue about tribal politics.

"Ross and his followers have no right to voice their opinions about anything that goes on here. They should be happy the Old Settlers let them live here at all!"

Grey sneered, and his visage darkened. "The Old Settlers should know John Ross is still our Chief, and he and his men have every right to say what they think about what goes on around here!"

Ben looked bewildered. "Would you please speak in English instead of Cherokee? When you talk fast, I don't understand all you say."

Through clenched teeth Grey spit out the English. "I only speak English to white people. Have you turned white, Ben?"

First Ben glared at Grey, and then he shook his head. This time he spoke softly in Cherokee. "No, I am not white, and I know that a young Cherokee shouldn't be speaking to an elder the way you are speaking to me."

Grey dropped his head in shame. "I am sorry, Cousin. I had no right to talk to you that way. You and Molly have been good to Blue and me, and I appreciate it."

Ben slapped him on the back and fell back into halting Cherokee. "That's all right, boy. I was the same way when I was your age. I thought I was right about everything back then, and I loved to argue to prove I was right. Marryin Molly and movin here has changed me. I had to change. That red-headed woman of mine and the folks around here wouldn't let me stay the same. You will understand what I mean when you get married and live here for a while. Why, I have had similar arguments with my two sons, and they don't even agree with each other! Marcus isn't much older than you, and he's a Ross man, too. You haven't met him because he is off attendin school back East and seldom gets home. I hope you can meet my older son Jacob at Christmas. Him and Fannie and their children are supposed to be here then. He is like me, an Old Settler, through and through. The two of you will probably knock heads all right."

"It will be good to meet them both."

"There's one thing I need to warn you. Try to stay out of local politics. Sayin the wrong thing to the wrong people can get you killed. I know some keep hollerin about the Cherokee blood law, and the clans are all riled-up about getting revenge. The Ross faction has put a thousand-dollar price on the heads of Tom Starr and his brothers for slaughterin so many of their people. It's said he's even killed the children of Ross supporters, burned houses, and stolen slaves. But don't forget what started all the bloodshed. When Ross supporters killed the Ridge, they killed a great Cherokee, not to mention his son John and nephew Elias Budinot. I knew all three men, and none of them deserved to be murdered."

"Some say they were executed for committing treason by unlawfully signing the Treaty of New Echota."

"Yes, that's the blood law comin into play. They say that, but others say they was just lookin out for the interest of the Cherokees when they signed it. They knew Jackson was goin to get his way in the end, and they might as well save themselves and other Cherokees while they could. Then the money they was offered no doubt influenced their decision to sign as well. Of course, some of us Old Settlers figured that out before they did and came to this land on our own."

"I don't blame you or any of our people for coming here early, but I will never accept what the treaty signers did."

Ben offered Grey some tobacco, which he declined. He placed a large chunk in his jaw and chewed. Spitting into the large bronze spittoon at his feet, he turned to face Grey again. "You don't have to accept it, Grey. Just don't voice your opinion. Don't speak for or against Ross or Watie in public. You never know who is kin to who around here and who might take offense and add your name to the list to be killed."

"Isn't that acting like a coward?"

"No, that's actin like a smart man and stayin alive so you can take care of your family."

Blue had been sitting by Grey's side, listening closely to the conversation. "Grey, I think you need to listen to your cousin."

Grey looked down at her and smiled. "It's hard not to hate those who wrong those you love. I would like to make them pay, but I will think about what you say, Ben. Blue, will you take a walk with me before it is bedtime?"

"All right, Grey."

Molly came into the room in time to hear their plans. "Don't forget your shawl. The air is nippy tonight. Grey, be sure you get her back to the house before it gets plumb dark. Oh, and I noticed that the loft is getting a bit messy. Do you think you can pick up all of your clothes and bring them down to the kitchen tonight, so we can include them in the washin tomorrow?"

"I can help him."

"Now, Blue, it wouldn't be proper for a young girl to be in an unmarried young man's sleepin quarters. No, Grey will take care of it hisself, and you will get settled in your trundle bed before Ben and me go to bed."

"All right, Molly."

Grey waited until they were out of earshot and chuckled. "Wonder what Molly would say if she knew you and I slept side by side near the fire for almost a month?"

"She would not be happy to hear that. Of course, that was back when I thought of you as my brother."

Grey took her small brown hand and enclosed it between his larger, darker hands. "And who do you think I am now?"

"My future husband."

"Yes, and you are my future wife." He drew her to himself and bent down so that his lips brushed hers.

Blue shivered, and he drew back. He placed his finger under her chin and raised her head so he could look into her eyes. "Did you know your eyes are the color of honey? I am sorry, Blue. You aren't ready to be kissed."

"You mean I don't have frog eyes anymore?"

"No, your eyes are amber colored, like honey, but sometimes when you are sad or mad, they turn dark. They never looked like frog eyes anyway. I just said that to tease you. Now let's walk around and listen to the whippoorwills. They sound just like the ones back home."

"Grey, you know there is one thing here I like better than at home."

"What's that?"

"The stars."

Grey lifted his head and surveyed the heavens. "The stars are just the same there as they are here."

Blue looked up at the starry sky. "Maybe, but you can see more of them here. The mountains at home blocked our view of the stars."

Grey looked again. "You know, I think you are right. And they are very bright tonight."

"Grey?"

"Yes?"

"I am ready for that kiss now."

BLUE'S THOUGHTS REMAINED focused on her future marriage to Wolf, so what happened three years later took her completely by surprise. Ben, Grey, and the hired hands had gone to Tahlequah for supplies. Blue was out back, helping Molly with the wash when the dogs started barking at the sound of galloping hoof beats. Molly finished wringing the water out of another pair of overalls and hung them on the line. "Now who could that be, ridin up in such a hurry? Run to the front of the house and see what is going on."

Before she reached the front porch, two rough-looking strangers were banging on the front door. Blue hid in some nearby bushes, waiting to see what the men wanted.

The shorter older man hitched his pants up and spat out a stream of brown tobacco juice. "Now ain't we lucky? Don't look like nobody's home so reckon we can just take what we want. Let's start with the livestock."

The younger man beat the barking dogs with the barrel of his rifle, and they yelped and slunk away. "Shut yur mouths! That's good, Pa, but you know I seen them Injuns in town one day, and they had a real purty squaw with them. I been thinkin about gettin me some of that all week. You know their wagon we saw on the road didn't have no women in it. Bet she's around here somewheres."

Blue's blood turned to ice, but she had to warn Molly before she could hide herself. Blue inched her way out of her hiding place.

"Now, we don't have time for that foolishness. You come help me with the cattle."

Blue had just emerged from the bushes when a big, dirty hand grabbed her ankle. "Well, speak of the devil! Here's that purty gal now!"

Blue screamed, kicked, and scratched, but he tossed her across his back like a bag of potatoes. "Settle down, sugar. Pa, me and this little gal have some bedroom business to attend to."

"Well, hurry it up! I can't do it all on my own."

"Oh, it won't take us long, will it, sugar?"

Blue struggled to get away. "Let me go! They will kill you if you hurt me."

"Now, ain't you the smart one! You can even speak English. Too bad it ain't your brain I'm after."

A few minutes later Blue was tossed in the middle of Ben and Mollie's bed. She jumped up and tried to crawl off but was quickly pushed back down. She felt her clothes being ripped apart. Yellow eyes, peering out of a grimy face, surveyed her nakedness with approval. "You're even purtier than I thought you would be. Bet you feel even better than you look."

Blue bit the finger that touched her breast and hung on, nearly gagging at the taste of the blood pouring into her mouth. "You're goin to pay for that! "Then he punched her in the face.

Blue struggled to move, but the heavy body pressed her flat. There was nothing she could do, and tears rolled down her face.

A shot rang out, and the big, bloody body stopped moving.

Molly yanked at the corpse. "Are you all right, Bluebird? Help me get this monster off of you. You push up, and I'll pull. Hurry now. I saw the other one in the barn, but if he heard the shot, he'll be here in a minute."

Working together, they shoved the body off the bed, and Molly helped the shaking girl to her feet. She swaddled Blue in a quilt and asked, "Did he rape you, Bluebird?"

"No, but he would have if you hadn't stopped him. Thank you."

"Well, I am glad of that. Now come on, we need to get out of here before the other one comes."

No sooner had she finished speaking when they heard yelling. "Bud, where did you get to? Thought I heard a shot. Did you kill the squaw?" Molly pushed Blue behind her and readied her weapon. As the man entered the room, she shot him, dead center in the forehead, and he fell like a stone.

Blue gasped. "Where did you learn to shoot like that?"

"Ben taught me. He said I needed to know how to defend myself in case he wasn't around to take care of me. We have guns hid all over the place. I'll show you where they are, and I'll teach you how to shoot."

Molly walked over to the younger corpse and kicked it. "I got this one in the back of the head. Ben always says to aim for the head, so that's what I do. Hand me the quilts off of the bed, so I can cover the bodies."

Blue's troubled eyes stared at her. "Molly, how are we going to explain these two dead white men at your house? Won't we get in trouble with the law?"

"Don't worry, honey. Ben and Grey will be back soon, and we'll come up with a solution for the problem. Now go downstairs, wash up, and put on some clean clothes. I'll tidy up here."

Blue couldn't stop trembling, and Molly ordered her to rest on the parlor sofa. Blue watched her friend calmly go about her daily routine. "Molly, how can you do it?"

"Do what, honey?"

"Act like nothing has happened."

"Nothing important has happened, Bluebird. You're still intact, and nothing has been stolen. All that has happened is two bad men have been punished for their sins. Can you help me move these brutes where they can't be seen? Then I'll fix you some tea, and you can sleep in our bed."

The tea worked, and Blue woke up in Grey Wolf's arms. He stroked her hair as she sobbed in his chest. "Are you all right, Blue?"

"I'm all right, just a little shaky."

"I am sorry, dear one. It is my fault. I shouldn't have left you alone."

"I wasn't alone. Molly was here."

"And I thank the Creator for that. I will never say a bad word about that woman again."

"Yes, she is wonderfully strong, but, Grey, what are we going to do about the bodies?"

"For now, nothing, until the hired hands go home. They seem like good men, but they aren't blood, and we can't put our trust in them. Now, come, Molly has supper ready, and you need to eat."

Blue could only manage a few bites of fried venison and gravy. Supper was quiet, and faces were grave. After the table was cleared, Ben stood to his feet and said, "Let's go talk in the parlor."

Ben stirred the coals in the fireplace, lit the coal oil lamp, and placed it on the table that sat in the center of the small, comfortable room. The room was so quiet that Blue could hear the clicking of Molly's knitting needles and the ticking of the marble clock on the mantle. No one uttered a word until Blue asked, "Are we going to get in trouble over what happened?"

Ben stood up and walked to where Blue was sitting on the brown settee beside Grey. He leaned over and gave her a reassuring hug. "No one's gettin in trouble because no one besides us knows what happened."

"Won't people come looking for those men?"

Ben snorted. "Men like them come to Indian Territory to get lost. Nobody knows they're here."

"How about the law? Aren't they looking for these bad men?"

Ben returned to his big chair and lit his pipe. "There ain't no real law in Indian Territory."

Grey spoke carefully so that Molly could understand his English. "We are Indians, and they were white. Wouldn't the soldiers at Fort Gibson care about that?"

Ben took a big puff and slowly blew it out. "They might if they knew, but they ain't goin to know. Me and you are goin to bury them bodies way out in the woods where no one will ever find them, and that will be the end of it. And we need never speak of it again."

Molly put down her knitting and smiled. "See there, Blue. I told you there was nothin to worry about."

The next day Molly added marksmanship to Blue's list of lessons. That night, when they were walking in the moonlight, Grey suddenly stopped and drew Blue over to a big tree stump and seated himself beside her. "Do you still want to know how I killed those soldiers on the trail? If you do, I will tell you because now I think you will understand why I did what I did."

"If you want to tell me, I would like to know."

"You remember the first time the Lieutenant gave us permission to trap rabbits?"

"Yes, I remember."

"I didn't turn my knife back in. I told them I lost it. They searched me and all my belongings and couldn't find it so they believed me. I had given it to Strong Bear to keep until I needed it. After Raven was attacked, I got it back. Strong Bear and I slipped off from the camp that night and tracked the two soldiers. They hadn't got far from our camp. He held them down while I slit their throats while they slept. I took the locks of hair from their heads, the watch, and the pipe. Then we threw the bodies and the knife down into a ravine."

"How did you get Raven's locket?"

"That was easy. Strong Bear's sister was a friend of Raven's, and she stole it for him."

"All right, but one thing I don't understand. How did you know we would be camped near the willow where you hid the locket and the other things?"

"I took a big chance when I did that. It was the only time I slipped off when it was still light. I waited until all the soldiers were busy setting up camp, and I just walked off. I found the willow, hid the locket and the soldiers' belongings there, and told you what to do that evening."

He took her hands in his and turned the palms upward. He kissed her palms and raised the cuffs of her sleeves so he could kiss her wrists and her arms. "Forgive me, Blue, for not being here to guard you from the white man's filthy hands. I could not have forgiven myself if he had raped you."

Blue felt dampness on her exposed skin and reached up to touch the tears falling from Grey's eyes. "Don't cry, Grey. You aren't to blame for what happened."

She used her handkerchief to dry his eyes, kissing his forehead and lips. "I have always loved you, Grey, but I want you to promise me something."

"What is that?"

"Promise me you will forget about the killing and the violence that was done on the Trail and is still being done in this new land. Promise me you will not bring it into our married life."

"I will do my best, but I will kill anyone who tries to harm you."

"And I would do the same. What I am talking about is don't get caught up in all this talk of blood law and revenge between the Ross faction and the treaty signers. I know you blame the treaty signers, and you hate them and the whites for what we went through on the Trail. But if we are to have peace, you must forget all that."

"It's hard, Blue, but I will do my best."

THREE YEARS HAD passed since they had finished the Trail. It had been three years of hard work, saving every penny, and learning to adapt to a new environment and new relationships. Grey and Blue still missed the beautiful mountains of their childhood, but they had grown accustomed to the smaller, green hills of what was called Indian Territory. Out of necessity, they had become fluent in English, but they still spoke Cherokee to each other and with other Cherokees. They announced that they would marry in Blue's sixteenth year.

When they were planning the wedding, Grey told Molly, "I will agree to marrying Blue in your church by your preacher as long as you agree to let me end the wedding in the Cherokee way."

Molly looked at Ben for guidance "It's their weddin, Molly, not yours. If they want part of it to be Cherokee, then so be it."

The morning of the wedding after Molly fastened the delicate hooks that held the white satin and lace dress together, she said, "Turn around and let me look at you." When Blue turned to face her, she just stared for a minute and said, "I never realized until now just how beautiful a woman you have become, my girl. Now all you need is a little accessory. Here you can wear these." She fastened a string of white pearls around Blue's slender neck.

"Ben gave me those on our first anniversary when we still lived in North Carolina. I kept them all these years, thinking I would give them to a daughter, but they were meant for you." She kissed Blue on the cheek. "Now off you go. It's time for the weddin."

When Ben walked down the aisle with the beautiful, golden-eyed girl, her black, shining hair falling to the small of her back, he caught a glimpse of the dazed bridegroom. "Bluebird, you have surely bewitched that poor boy."

Blue looked up at him and giggled. "Stop teasing me, Ben."

Then she looked at Grey and realized Ben was right. Grey was looking at her like he had never seen her before. Did she really look that different?

The first part of the ceremony was conducted in the community church that Ben and Molly attended by their pastor, Brother Brown. Bluebird usually accompanied them to Sunday services, but despite Molly's entreaties, Grey never went. After Brother Brown proclaimed them to be man and wife, they walked down the aisle out the front door. They were met by a small, elderly Cherokee man, who prayed over them in Cherokee for several minutes.

Molly poked Ben in the ribs and whispered, "What is he sayin?"

"He's just blessin them and their marriage."

Grey and the elder nodded at each other, and Grey said, "Wa-do."

The older man laughed and congratulated Grey on finding a pretty woman. Then he turned to Blue, smiled, and introduced himself. "Pathseeker."

"*Wa-do*, Pathseeker."

After he and Grey spoke a few more minutes, Pathseeker waved, and walked away. They joined Ben and Molly in their buggy and went back to their house to eat lunch and pack their belongings. On their wedding day, they were moving to a ramshackle cabin on a tiny farm in the small community of Jubilee.

As they enjoyed the special wedding cake she had baked for them, Molly tried once more to change their plans. "I don't know why you don't just stay here. You could sleep in the loft until Ben can build a room onto the house, and you would have your own private place. You don't know about those people in Jubilee who promised you could live on their land and be their sharecroppers. They might let you live there until you harvest their crops, and, then as soon as they no longer need you, boot you out on the road. Then what will you do?"

"Now, Molly, you can't keep them here forever. You're not Blue's mother, even though you act like it. They want to get out on their own and make a new life for theirselves." Ben turned where Molly couldn't see and winked at Grey

Grey returned the wink and turned back to Molly. "Thanks for understanding. We do want to thank you for all you have done for us, but it is time for us to leave."

Blue hugged Molly. "We will never forget your kindness."

Molly blinked back tears. "I know. I guess it's because we only had boys that you seem like my daughter. But, please, Jubilee isn't that far away so you can come back and see us anytime."

"We will. I promise to wash this beautiful wedding dress you loaned me and return it to you next Sunday. She pointed at the pearls which graced her neck. "You should also take these pearls back. They are too fine for me."

"Oh, don't worry about that. I don't know anyone else that can wear the dress except you. It sure won't fit me anymore! Just keep it and the pearls. They are both wedding gifts. But I will hold you to your promise to come see us next Sunday and eat dinner with us."

Blue turned to Grey for agreement, and he gave a quick nod. "Yes, we will do that, Molly. I will bring a cake or pie for dessert."

"No need for that. Just come and eat with us."

Grey patted Molly's arm. "All right then. We better get on the road. Come on, Blue."

Grey offered his hand and helped Blue up into the wagon, which was loaded down with everything they owned, most of which had been given to them by Ben and Molly. When they got to the end of the lane that led to the Wolf house, Blue turned to wave goodbye.

Grey reached over and squeezed her knee. "We will be at our new home in a little while, Blue. Will you be glad to get there?"

"Yes. Will you?"

"Oh, yes!"

Grey grinned and gave her a quick kiss.

AFTER HE HELPED Blue down from the wagon, Grey put his hands on her shoulders and said, "I know it is run-down, but I will fix it up. I came here yesterday evening and cleaned a little. Be careful where you step. I promise to nail those boards on the porch in the morning. You go on inside, and I will unload the wagon."

"Don't you need my help?"

"No. I can manage most of it, and we can wait on the rest of it until tomorrow. You go inside and get ready for bed."

"But it's not dark yet."

His black eyes shone and danced. "We won't be sleeping. Now go wash the dust off and put on that pretty nightgown Molly gave you. The pump in the kitchen works fine."

Blue blushed. "Oh, all right."

A few minutes later Grey was standing by the bed, looking down at Blue, who was lying on the bed. "You look so beautiful!"

"Not like a frog?"

"No, not a bit."

He unbuttoned his suspenders, dropped his overalls, removed his shirt, and slowly took off his underwear. For the first time, Bluebird saw the proof of Grey's masculinity. Then he took Bluebird into his arms and made her his woman.

Bluebird had thought she knew what hard work was at Ben and Molly's house, but she soon learned she had been mistaken. She had cooked eggs and ham, sent by Molly, for breakfast on the old wood stove, and they were still unloading the heavy items from the wagon the next morning when they heard a horse approaching. The landowner they would be working for, Nick Sanders, dismounted and tied his horse's reins to a nearby tree. "Howdy, folks! I thought you two would be out workin in the fields this mornin."

Grey frowned, and Bluebird held her breath, but he spoke up in English. "Sorry, sir. We planned on getting to it as soon as we got our belongings in place."

"Now that's not goin to do. You need to get up early, eat, and get in the fields before the sun starts shinin down."

"We will do better tomorrow, sir. We just got here yesterday afternoon."

"Well, see that you do. Now I'll leave you to it, but I will be back tomorrow to see what you got done."

The same pattern was repeated for several days. Nick came to check on their progress every morning. At first, he found fault. "You're goin to have to do more each day if them beans are goin to make."

Finally, they hit upon a scheme to meet his standards. Blue would get up before daylight and cook breakfast. She would cook enough biscuits and meat so they had leftovers for lunch. After eating quickly, Grey would take his hoe or other tool and go out to the fields while Blue pumped water to wash the morning dishes. Then she would join Grey in the fields. They would stop at midday for a quick snack on the leftovers and resume working until nearly dark. Blue would stop a few minutes before Grey, go to the house and fry some more meat and eggs in their iron skillet. He would soon join her, and they would eat in an exhausted daze. Then he would wash up and go to bed while she washed the dishes and did necessary housework. The next day their routine would be repeated, and repeated again throughout the week.

Their only relief was Sunday when Nick and his family went to church and then stayed home all day. After keeping their promise to Molly to come for Sunday dinner their first week of married life, they explained they wouldn't be back for some time. On Sundays Blue cleaned house, did their laundry, and cooked meals while Grey checked on the fields, often doing necessary chores there, and made needed repairs to improve their small house.

After a month, the owner came by and said, "Now that's more like it. You finally got the hang of it. Tomorrow I will bring you a cow and a few chickens. That way you won't have to wait on me to bring you milk and eggs for cookin."

"Thank you, sir. We appreciate it."

Nick grabbed Grey's hand and shook it. "That's all right, young man, and you can call me Nick. That's my name. See you in the mornin."

Bluebird was relieved when, after checking to make sure that they were taking proper care of the cow and chickens, Nick limited his inspection visits to once a week. They still worked as hard, or perhaps even harder, since milking, feeding, and gathering eggs were new tasks added to her list, but they somehow managed to find time to be together for talks and love making.

A year later Bluebird was gathering wood for the small campfire Grey had built when she looked up to see a falling star streak across the night sky. She felt a stirring and a fluttering in her belly. "Grey, something wonderful just happened!"

Grey looked up from stirring the fire. "What is it?"

"I felt the baby kick, and then I saw a star fall from the sky."

Grey walked over and put his arm around her. "Do you think it might be a sign?"

"Yes, I think the baby should be named Tlun-dah-chee for the star that fell. What do you think?"

"I like that. It would be good for a boy or a girl, even though, we know it will be a boy."

"I don't know that."

"I do."

But Grey was wrong. Star came into the world, fighting, fists flailing, legs kicking. "Like a little mad bee! That's what you should have named her," said Molly.

Bluebird, weak from loss of blood, mumbled, "No, she's Star."

Grey looked with concern at his wife's pale face. He asked the weary Cherokee midwife, Kohene Fivekiller, who had delivered Star, "Is she going to be all right, healer?

"Yes, in time. But I must give her a tea that will keep her from getting pregnant again, which she must drink every morning. Another baby could kill her."

"Do what you must as long as Blue is all right."

Molly said, "I will keep this little bee for you until Blue is able," and she swaddled the baby in layers of warm white cotton material.

It was two months before Kohene would allow Blue to get out of bed. When she finally approved, she said, "Yes, Bluebird, you can get out of bed and care for your baby but no hard work for another four months. I have never, in all my years of delivering babies, seen a harder delivery than yours."

She pinned back a lock of gray-streaked hair that had fallen out of the bun on top of her head and rubbed her tired dark eyes with her hand. "Now I am going home to get some rest. I was up until early this morning delivering Kate Christie's new baby. She lost two babies, but this boy looks healthy. Molly, make sure that Bluebird does what I told her to. Don't let her do anything but take care of her baby. I will be back to check on her at the end of the month."

"I will see to it, Kohene. Thank you. We don't mind a bit, do we, little Bee? All right, Bluebird, let me help you up from the chair, and you can hold your baby girl."

A FEW MONTHS later, Grey traveled to Sallisaw to the

saltworks which had once belonged to the respected Cherokee, Sequoyah, to buy some salt for their household. Grey had never seen salt made, so he spent some time looking at the giant salt kettles and asking questions. One of the workers carried out the bushels of salt that Grey purchased. The huge Cherokee reminded him of someone. Then the man turned and said, "Grey Wolf? Is that you?"

"Strong Bear?"

The two men laughed and clasped arms in greeting. "Follow me to my house, Grey."

"Can you leave this place when you are supposed to be working?"

"The boss isn't here today, and no one dares to tell on me. Besides, I will return after we have spoken."

Grey followed Strong Bear to a small neat cabin in the woods, about five miles from the saltworks. Around the porch three small boys played. The boys stopped and looked up at Grey. The oldest boy asked in Cherokee, "Who is he, Father?"

"This is my good friend, Grey Wolf. We came over on the Trail together. Now run and tell your mother we have a guest for dinner."

Then he turned to Grey and pointed with his chin. "You can unhitch your horses and water them at the trough over there. Just tie them up anywhere. There's plenty of trees to choose from. And if you need the outhouse, it's at the end of the path behind the house. Just make yourself at home and come inside when you're finished."

A few minutes later Grey Wolf was greeted by a pregnant Raven. She slapped him on the back. "Si-yo, Grey! It's been a long time. How are you and Blue doing?"

"Si-yo, Raven." Then he pointed at her belly and smiled. "It looks like you have been blessed."

"Yes, I have been blessed four times. Do you and Blue have any children yet?"

"Yes, we have one little girl."

"Oh, I would love to have a little girl, someone to dress up and teach the old ways. I hope this one is a girl."

Strong Bear put his arm around Raven. "It's probably another boy.

Boys run in my family. You know I have loved this one a long time, all the way from the Trail until we got here. We married in the Cherokee way right after the Trail. Our first one was born a few months after we settled here."

Raven removed his arm and scolded them. "Are you men going to stand here all day and talk, or do you want to eat? Your food is getting cold. Wash up at the pump in the kitchen and come to the table."

A few minutes later Grey smacked his lips and rubbed his stomach in appreciation. "This is very good food, Raven. I haven't had grape dumplings since Granny last made them for me."

"Doesn't Blue make you grape dumplings?"

"She would if she knew how. I don't think her mother taught her to cook much, and my cousin's wife Molly taught her to cook in the white way. Her food is good, though, just not Cherokee food."

Raven ladled another helping of grape dumplings in his plate. "Bring her to see me, and I will teach her to cook the Cherokee way."

"Maybe I will. Blue complains about missing her friends from the Trail. About the only woman she ever visits is our neighbor, Kate Christie, who was Kate Springwater on the Trail. But Kate isn't one for visiting. She is quite a bit older than Blue and has a reputation of being a shrewd business woman. I have heard her husband spends his time finding horses for her to trade and sell."

After the meal was over, Strong Bear said, "Come outside. I want to show you something."

Strong Bear led him to a corral where a young bay stallion eyed them. "Nice horse. Is he what you wanted to show me?"

"No, I just wanted to talk where Raven couldn't hear. What do you know about James and Tom Starr?"

"I know James, Tom's father, signed an illegal treaty. I heard that Tom has a price on his head, but no one has collected on it yet."

"Did you know that every time James hears a rumor that someone is going to kill him he runs to Fort Gibson for protection?"

"No, I didn't know that. Does that mean the Ross supporters have given up on getting revenge?"

Strong Bear scowled and huffed. "What do you think?"

"They still plan to kill him. How about Tom?"

"He murders people because they threaten his father or disagree with his politics. It's said he wears an ear lobe from each man he kills on a necklace around his neck. You came over the Trail. What do you think about the treaty signers?"

"What they did wasn't right."

"It was more than that. It was treason."

"Yes, I would agree with you."

"If you agree, you can meet me and some others tomorrow morning on the road by James Starr's house. His house isn't too far from Jubilee. We are going to kill him for signing the treaty, and all the Starr males who are there, including Tom. It's good luck we met today. I have seen you kill men who deserved to die, and I know you will help us kill others who deserve the same fate."

Grey dropped his eyes and shook his head. "No, Strong Bear, I have made a promise to not kill again, unless it is in defense of someone I love."

Strong Bear scoffed. "What is this soft woman's talk of love? Where is that hard strong wolf I knew on the Trail?"

"I don't know. Perhaps he is lost."

"Find the wolf and bring him back. The Wolf clan has always defended our people. It is your duty to help your people rid ourselves of the traitors who live in our midst. I will see you tomorrow morning by James Starr's house."

"I will think on it."

"Then you will be there. I am glad we got to talk, but it's time I got back to work."

"And it's time I go home. *Wa-do* for the good food. Goodbye."

AS THEY WERE eating supper, Grey told Blue about his chance encounter with Strong Bear and Raven. "Oh, can we go and see them soon? It's been so long since I have talked to Raven, and I would love to see her little boys. I could put Star in that new pink dress Molly made her, the one with all the ruffles and lace. Maybe we could go see them on Saturday unless Strong Bear has to work. If he does, we can go on Sunday."

"Strong Bear has plans for the next few days."

"We could visit some other time."

"Maybe."

Blue paused in spooning gravy into Star's little mouth. The baby's mouth changed into a surprised little "o", and she let out an outraged wail. "Hush, Star. Why don't you want to visit them? You know how much I miss Raven and the other girls from the Trail."

"It depends on something else that might happen. I will tell you when I know."

Blue frowned at him and went back to feeding the baby.

When the morning came, Grey arose extra early to feed and water the stock. The baby awoke and fussed so Blue got up to care for her. She found Grey in the parlor cleaning his rifle. Just as she and the baby entered the room, Grey jumped up and hurriedly assembled his rifle. "Someone's coming. You and Star hide in the bedroom."

"What's wrong?"

"Just do what I say. I'm going to see who it is."

She looked out the bedroom window and saw two riders dismount and stand on the porch talking with Grey. One of them was big and looked like Strong Bear. The next minute Grey burst into the room and started rummaging through the trunk. Blue shifted Star to the other hip and stood in front of Grey. "What are you looking for? Is that Strong Bear?'

"I am looking for my extra ammunition. And yes, it is Strong Bear."

"I want to talk to him." She started to leave the room, but Grey grabbed her arm and held her back.

"Not now. We are going hunting, and Strong Bear is in a hurry to be off."

"Surely there is time to say *si-yo*."

His face was a mask of worry and anger. "No! You must trust me, all right?"

"All right, but I will have a lot of questions for you when you come home tonight."

"I will answer all of them." He grabbed the pouch of bullets from the trunk and gave her and Star a light kiss.

The baby fussed, and Blue patted her back to calm her down. Then she stood at the window, watching the three men ride away.

Blue did her usual cooking and cleaning, including boiling the family's laundry outside in a large iron pot. After waiting until nearly dark, she ate supper alone.

After supper, Blue gave Star a bath in a tin tub on the kitchen table. She laughed as the baby cooed and kicked her little feet, splashing water out of the tub. "You are making a mess, little girl. Just wait until your papa gets home. I will tell him all about your bad behavior."

Blue sighed, took the wet baby out of the water, and wrapped her up in a blanket. She laid her on the bed and dressed her in a fresh gown and diaper. "There that's better. Where is your daddy tonight, Star?"

Feeling uneasy, Blue made sure the heavy bar was in place to lock the front door. Even though it was barely dark, she felt drained and yearned for a few minutes of oblivion. She lay down beside Star and listened to the baby's soft breathing. Where was Grey? Had he gotten himself in trouble with Strong Bear and the other man?

Blue nodded off but was soon jarred out of sleep by a loud knocking at the door. She got up and walked to the window to look out. By the moonlight, she could see Grey standing by the door. Blue ran to the front door, raised the bar, and admitted her haggard husband.

"Come in and have something to eat. I kept some stew warm on the hearth for you. Sit and eat."

Noticing Gray's trembling hands, she grabbed a quilt from the bed and threw it over his shoulders. "Are you cold? What's wrong?"

Grey let her to help him sit down, but he still wasn't talking. Blue's eyes grew big and fearful, and she placed the back of her hand across his forehead. "You don't have a fever, but you look sick. Can you talk?"

Grey's voice was harsh and low. "I can talk, but I don't want to right now. Just let me eat something and go to bed. I will tell you what happened in the morning. Can you keep your questions until then?"

"Yes. Of course, I can."

Blue watched Grey sleeping. She felt safer now he was home, but she dreaded hearing what he would say to her in the morning. She knew something terrible had happened.

Grey got up, did all his chores, and ate breakfast with Blue and Star. He smiled at Star when she cooed at him but spoke very little to Blue. Finally, in frustration, she asked, "Are you ever going to talk to me?"

"Soon."

Then there was a knock at the door, and Grey looked at her with fear in his eyes. "Quick, take Star into the bedroom!" She picked up the baby and started toward the bedroom when she heard Ben's voice.

"Grey, are you home?"

Grey threw the bar back, and Ben walked in. "Molly sent me over to check on you two. James Starr and his crippled son were killed yesterday by a bunch of men. She was afraid someone might have talked you into going over there."

A cold needle of ice pierced Blue's heart, and she gasped. "Is that where you were all day yesterday?"

"I was getting ready to tell you about it. It's all right. I didn't go to the house. I'm glad I didn't. I could never kill a crippled man."

Ben spoke up. "I heard he wasn't a man, just a boy, and they shot him in front of his mother."

"Well, I sure wouldn't do that. How about Tom Starr?"

"They say he wasn't there, but one of his brothers escaped and got him word. He's vowed to kill every man who took part in the killing. I just hope no one tells him you were there."

Blue hugged herself to control her trembling. Her voice was a soft whisper. "The men you rode with, will they tell you were there?"

"Strong Bear would never talk, but I don't know about Badger."

Ben walked to the kitchen table and pulled out a chair. "Sit down, Grey. We need to talk. Tell me how this all started."

Blue looked down at the sleeping baby in her arms. "Let me go lay Star down. I want to hear what happened, too."

In a few minutes, Blue came back to the kitchen table with a tray, holding three cups of coffee for Ben, Grey, and herself. She sat down and fixed her eyes on Grey. "All right. Tell us."

Grey stirred sugar into his coffee and took a sip. Then he looked up at Ben. "Strong Bear told me about the plan the Ross supporters made to kill James Starr and his family. They wanted revenge for Starr's part in the treaty signing and for the murderous actions of his sons. He wanted me to help him and the others kill the Starrs. I told him I wasn't interested, and I could see he didn't believe me. Yesterday morning Strong Bear and his friend Badger showed-up here and told me they couldn't guarantee my family's safety if I didn't go with them. I grabbed my rifle and some extra ammunition and rode with them."

"They put you in a bad spot. What happened next?"

"On the way to Starr's, Strong Bear kept talking about the need to punish the treaty signers and their families. I said, 'I agree they did wrong, but I believe only the signers should pay for their crime. You're talking about killing every male in James Starr's family, and that doesn't seem right.'"

"But he kept saying, 'The sons are just as dangerous as the fathers. Tom Starr has said he will kill anyone who says anything against his father, and his brothers feel the same way. We will wipe out a nest of snakes tonight and give a message to the rest of the traitors to get out of Indian Territory or stay and be killed.'"

"How about this Badger? What did he say?"

"He didn't say much. Just laughed at me when I jumped as an owl flew into Winter's face and spooked him. I believe he made a joke about never seeing a wolf afraid of an owl before. I knew it was a sign I should come back home, but I ignored it. The only other time he spoke he threatened to shoot me when I wouldn't take part in the killing."

Blue rocked back and forth in her chair. Grey reached out and put his hand on her shoulder to steady her. "It's all right, Blue. I am fine."

Blue quit rocking, but she grimaced. "For now."

Ben sipped his coffee and looked over at Grey. "Finish the story."

"By the time we got there, there must have been twenty or more men, waiting for the signal to go in. I figured I could just ride off, and no one would know I was gone. Badger saw me, though, and announced I was a coward and a traitor. He started pushing me around, and the leader told him and another man to tie me to a tree, and they would deal with me later. Strong Bear waited until they had all ridden off, and he untied me. He told me to just give him the extra ammunition, and he would act surprised when they came back and discovered I was gone. He said he owed me that much for how I had helped Raven on the Trail. As I was riding away, I heard gun shots and screams. I rode hard because I didn't know when they might set off after me."

Blue wiped her eyes and blew her nose. "Why did it take you so long to get home?"

"I kept backtracking in case anyone followed me, and I have been hiding out in the woods for hours now, waiting for the dark. I wanted to make sure no one could track me to this house."

Grey put his head in his hands and sobbed. After a few minutes, he stopped crying and looked up at his cousin, "What should I do, Ben?"

Ben leaned over and patted Grey on the back. "Well, first off, you gotta lay low for a while until all of this has blowed over. Tom has vowed to kill every man who had anything to do with his kin's deaths."

Blue gasped. "We can't let him kill Strong Bear and Raven!"

Ben patted Blue's hand. "I can send a letter by one of the hands to Sallisaw to warn them."

"Please do. They are our friends, and Strong Bear probably saved Grey's life."

Ben finished his coffee and stood up. "All right. I'll go home and send word to the saltworks for Strong Bear. Grey, you must give me your word you will stay at your house until I tell you it is safe to leave."

Grey nodded. "I promise."

"All right then. I will send over Gene to keep guard. He's a good man to have around when you need a good shot with a steady hand and head, and he's an Old Settler, so I trust him."

In the days that followed Ben carried them word that Tom Starr, his brothers, and cohorts boasted to have murdered over half of the men involved in the deaths of James and Buck Starr. "President Polk himself is threatenin to step in, and most of the treaty party have moved off, some to Arkansas, some below the Red River, and some to other parts of Indian Territory. Tom's set up residence near Briartown, in Creek country."

Blue asked, "How about Strong Bear and Raven?"

"Last I heard they was headin out West somewhere."

Grey looked into Ben's eyes. "Do you think we are really safe now?"

"I think so, but be on your guard."

"I always am."

FOUR YEARS LATER, Grey was buying supplies at a store in Tahlequah. Star had begged him to take her with him, and he had given in. She was chattering in Cherokee and running all over the store, excited about all the toys and candies that were on display. Grey was busy talking to the proprietor about what he wanted to buy and lost track of her. He looked up from the counter to hear a tall, mixed-blood speaking Cherokee.

"What's your name, pretty girl?"

Star looked up and grinned. "My name's Star."

The man laughed and patted her cheek. "Well, how about that? My name's Starr, too, Tom Starr. Pleased to meet you, pretty Star."

Grey overheard the conversation. He called to Star, "Come here, Star. Don't be bothering people."

She ran to where her father was, and Tom followed her. Their eyes met, and Tom said, "Do I know you?"

Grey shook his head. "No, I don't think so. We don't come to town much. My name is Grey Wolf."

Tom's eyes turned dark and cold, and he frowned a minute. Then he held out his hand. "Well, I'm Tom Starr. I used to live around these parts, but I just came home for a visit to see my kinfolks. You sure have a pretty little girl."

Grey took his hand and said in Cherokee what he had heard white men say. "Pleased to meet you."

Star tugged at his sleeve. "Will you buy me something to play with?"

Grey looked down at her. "You know we don't have much money left over, but I will buy you some candy."

Tom said, "Well, looky here, Miss Star. Look and see what I found on the floor."

He held out his hand and showed her a dime. "Would you like to have it?"

Star plucked it from his hand. "Yes, I would! *Wa-do.*" Then she ran over to the shelf that contained the toys.

Grey smiled at Tom. "You didn't have to do that, but it was very kind of you."

Tom's eyes turned cold again, and he said, "Maybe today is a day for kindness. Take care of that pretty girl, Grey Wolf."

WHEN GREY TOLD Blue about his encounter with Tom Starr, she shivered. "Do you think he will come here?"

"I don't think so. I heard that leaders of the Ross faction and the treaty signers signed a truce to stop killing each other, and all past acts of violence would be pardoned."

"So, Tom Starr will never have to pay for the people he killed?"

"It doesn't look like it."

"That doesn't seem right, but I don't care. As long as he doesn't bother anyone I love, I won't worry about what happens to him."

Star grew to be an intelligent, strong-willed child, with long, glossy hair that hung to her waist and dark flashing eyes like her father. By the time she turned eight, they had bought the small house and acreage they had been living on, and she began playing with some white children whose parents had bought Nick's home place. One day she came home after a day of playing with her new friends and announced, in English, "I want to go to school tomorrow."

Grey frowned at her and said in Cherokee, "Why are you speaking in the white tongue? Talk in Cherokee."

"Why can't I talk in English? That's what my friends and I talk. Polly Clay and her brother Sam don't know Cherokee."

She changed to Cherokee when Grey began to scowl. "All right, but may I go to school tomorrow? They said that they would stop by for me."

"You don't need to go to that school. Your mother will teach you everything you need to learn."

Blue spoke up, "I think it might be good for Star to go to school."

"Why would you think that?"

"She needs to learn how to read and write."

"I can teach her how to use Sequoyah's syllabary for that, the way I taught you."

"Yes, you should do that, but I think learning in English would be good, too."

"Cherokee is good enough for you and me, and it is good enough for our daughter."

"Times are changing, Grey. All of the Cherokee families in Jubilee are sending their children to the mission school to learn along with the white children. Do you want our girl to be the only one who can't use English to read, write, and cipher? Learning is a good thing, and I want good things for Star."

"No, I still don't like the idea."

"*Please*, Father."

Grey's eyes turned black. "You heard me."

Star sobbed and ran to her room. For several mornings she stood at the window and watched as her friends walked to school. Blue tried to talk to Grey about the matter, but nothing she said would change his mind. Then one evening a visitor knocked at their front door.

Blue opened the door to an attractive young Cherokee woman. Her black hair was neatly braided into a bun, covered by a small, wide-brimmed straw hat, trimmed with a black ribbon. She was dressed in a white, high-necked blouse, trimmed in lace, tucked neatly into a black twill skirt. The young woman smiled warmly at Blue and after greeting her, continued to speak to her in Cherokee. "My name is Tsu-la Doublehead, and I am a new teacher at Jubilee School. I have heard there is a Cherokee child living here who might be interested in attending our school."

Blue laughed and grabbed Tsu-la's hands. "Tsu-la, don't you recognize me? It's Blue from the Trail."

Tsu-la's dark eyes got big and she giggled. "Blue, is it really you? Where's Grey? Is he here with you?"

"Yes, he is. Grey, come here, and see an old friend."

Grey walked into the room and then stopped and stared. "Tsu-la, is that you? How did you get so grown-up?"

Tsu-la giggled again. "Me? Look at you and Blue! You're married and even have a child. May I meet her?"

Grey lightly slapped her shoulder. "Sure you can. Star, come here and meet one of our old friends."

Star walked in slowly, frowning, with her head down. Then she looked up and grinned when she saw Tsu-la. "Hello, Teacher. I haven't met you, but my friends, Polly and Sam told me all about you."

Grey looked at Star and shook his head. "Why don't you ever tell me these things? If you had said your teacher was Tsu-la, I would have gladly allowed you to attend school. I thought your teacher would be a stern old white woman who would try to turn you into a white girl."

Tsu-la patted Grey's hand. "I promise I will never try to turn any Cherokee child white. My goal is to teach them all I have learned from the whites. Star will not only learn how to speak and write English, but she will learn how to cipher and the geography and history of this world we all live in. Surely, you wouldn't forbid her from learning such valuable lessons?"

"No, I wouldn't forbid that because I trust you."

Star fairly quivered with excitement, and she gave her father a big hug. "Oh, I am so happy! Thank you, Pa."

"You're welcome, Star. Now, Tsu-la, come and sit with us. Blue, don't we have some cobbler left over from supper? Fix a bowl for Star's teacher."

Star was older than most of the beginning students, but she was a natural scholar and applied herself to learning to read and write. Within three months, she was moved into a group with other children her age. "

Grey complained. "Star always has her head in a book these days!"

"Leave her alone. She loves to read, and it's good for her. And I love the stories she tells from her books."

"Huh! She should be telling Cherokee stories."

"She knows those, too."

"Yes, but she seldom asks to hear one anymore, and I have to keep reminding her to talk in Cherokee when she's home."

"She just forgets."

Star called from the kitchen where she was snacking on cornbread and buttermilk. "I hear you two talking about me. It's hard to remember to talk Cherokee here when I talk English all the time at school and with my friends."

Grey called back. "Come in here and talk to me."

When Star came into the room with her bowl of food, he glared at her. "Maybe you should get some Cherokee friends."

"I have one Cherokee friend, Clara Turtle, but my best friend is Polly. She wants me to spend the night with her Saturday night and go to church with her Sunday. May I?"

"Maybe. If you get finished helping your mother with the laundry and get all your other chores done, you can go."

Star grinned, and her dark eyes shone. "I promise I will finish in record time."

When Star came home on Sunday, she greeted her mother with a question. "May I go back next Saturday night? I had so much fun, and I liked going to church."

"You don't need to go over there every Saturday. Why don't you ask Polly if she would like to come over here?"

Star rolled her eyes and sighed. "Ma, you don't understand. Polly wants to go to church every Sunday, and I do, too. I love the Sunday School class and the pretty music and songs. I love it all, except the preaching. That lasts too long, and it's hard to sit still that long."

"Why don't you ask your father if you can walk over to Polly's house on Sunday morning and go to church with them? Then you can walk back here from their house after church is over."

Suddenly Star was all smiles again. "Oh, that's a good idea, Ma! Do you think Pa will let me?"

"All you can do is ask."

Grey said no at first, but when Star came to him the second time, with tears in her eyes, he gave in, with one condition. "On the Saturday nights we stay late for stomp dances, you will stay home from church the next morning."

"May I go over and play at Polly's house sometime, and may she come over here?"

"I suppose that would be all right."

The first time the red-headed, freckled Polly came to play with Star, Grey smiled and greeted the child in English. As soon as he judged the girls were out of hearing distance, he whispered, "Poor little girl! She is so ugly!"

Blue frowned and hushed him. "Polly isn't ugly. You are just not used to being around little white girls."

When the two girls were laughing and squealing over something that had happened at school, Grey stopped to speak to Blue before leaving the house. "I think I am used to being around little white girls now. They may not be ugly, but they are certainly noisy."

The year Star turned ten, she came home with a big grin on her face and a huge book in her hands. "Look at what I got for winning the spelling bee today! It's a brand-new dictionary with all the words in the English language. Missus Doublehead says I put the older students to shame today."

Grey said, "Don't brag too much. Remember what happened to Opossum when he bragged on his beautiful tail?"

"I remember, Pa. Tsi-s-du tricked him, and his beautiful tail turned into the ugly, stringy one that opossums have today. But that is just an old story."

"Yes, but it is Cherokee, and it teaches a lesson."

"Well, this big book will teach me a lot of lessons, too, about English words."

Blue took the book from Star's hand and examined it. "This is a very nice book you won. May I borrow it sometime? I need to improve my English."

Grey just muttered something in Cherokee and walked off.

Life passed quickly and happily, and almost in a blink of an eye, Star was graduating from the mission school. Grey wasn't happy when Star announced she had agreed to take Tsu-la's teaching position. "Isn't it exciting, Pa? Missus Doublehead is finally going to have a baby, so, of course, she has to resign. She wrote a letter to the Mission Board, recommending me for the job."

Grey fumed. "Why do you want to waste your time trying to teach a bunch of white children who think they are better than you?"

"First of all, I am teaching both white and Cherokee children. Second, I have never heard any child say he or she is better than I. Third, and most important, I love to teach almost as much as I love to read, so I will be doing what makes me happy."

Grey threw his hands up and left the room. After sulking for a few days, he accepted Star's decision. But two years later Star made an announcement he couldn't accept.

Star wore a nervous smile as she knocked on their door that morning. After making small talk, she cleared her throat and only made eye contact with her mother. "I just came by to tell you Samuel Clay and I are getting married. We will be moving into Samuel's homeplace, which his parents left him when they passed away awhile back."

Star stopped speaking for a minute when she glimpsed the anger growing in her father's eyes. Turning completely away from him, she spoke to her mother, "I thought my parents would be happy with me living just across the field from them."

Grey put his hand up to stop her talking. "My daughter will never marry a white! You bring shame on your family by even considering such a thing. No, I will not allow it!"

Blue tried to calm him. "Grey, he is a good man, and he will be good to Star. You really can't forbid her to marry since she is a grown woman." Secretly Blue was relieved. She had known Sam since he was a young boy, and Star had always been close to his sister, Polly. She had heard only good things about Samuel Clay, the man, and she wanted her cherished daughter to have a good man at her side.

Speaking in Cherokee, Star said, "Father, I love you, but I also love Samuel Clay, and he loves me. We are going to be married, with or without your blessing."

Grey stopped in the middle of his morning ritual of combing out his long black hair before tying it back out of the way. He turned to look at Star. "Why would you marry an ugly, hairy white man?"

"I don't think he's ugly, and Sam is good and gentle, and he loves me very much."

Grey threw the comb on the floor and turned his fury loose on Blue. "See what letting her play and go to school with white children has led to? This is all your fault! If you marry this white man, you will leave my house, and I never want to see you again!"

"Samuel is waiting in his buggy, just down the lane. We are going to Brother Brown's house. He said he would marry us. Polly and her beau will stand up for us. I'm sorry, Mother, that you can't see me married. Father, I hope you change your mind. Goodbye."

For the first time in many years, Blue spoke to her husband in anger. "If you won't speak to our daughter, then I won't speak to you." Blue kept her promise. For several weeks, she silently placed Grey's meals on the table and took her own food outside where she ate it, silently. She slept in Star's old room and avoided her husband whenever possible. Finally, Grey had enough.

He came out to the front porch where Blue was sitting, mending the holes in his moccasins. "All right, Blue. You win. There is too much between us for us to remain apart. You know all of my secrets and all of my faults, yet you still love me. You can tell Star she can come back here and visit, but I don't want that white man here."

Blue stopped mending and looked up at him. "Yes, I know you, inside and out, and you know me. You know I won't be satisfied until you accept Sam, but this is a beginning. I will go see her today."

Months later a spring of heavy rains caused the many small streams to overflow their banks until ranchers and their hands spent most of their time rescuing their stock from the rising water. Grey was checking on his cows when he looked over at the adjoining pasture and saw Samuel Clay run and jump headfirst into a raging torrent. His curiosity aroused, Grey walked over to see what happening. There was Samuel Clay hanging on to an uprooted tree in the middle of a fast moving, powerful river. In the bend of his arm was a half-drowned Indian boy. "Help us, Grey Wolf!"

Grey spotted a nearby long, woody vine, took out his big sharp knife and hacked off a substantial piece. Grasping the vine, he braced himself at the foot of a sturdy sycamore tree and dug his heels in. Then he positioned himself so he could lower the vine down to where Samuel could reach out and grab it.

"Good thinkin. Better get the boy out first." Samuel shook the boy until he regained consciousness. Then he pantomimed what he wanted the boy to do.

"All right. Start pullin. He knows he's to hang on for dear life. Don't think you can pull me out, though."

Grey pushed his heels in deeper into the thick dark mud, strained, and pulled. Finally, he could see the boy as he emerged from the water and pulled himself up the bank to where Grey was standing. He shivered and shook himself off like a dog. Grey took off his jacket and put it on the boy. He looked up at Grey and said, *"Wa-do."*

Grey tapped him on the shoulder. "Can you speak English?"

"A little."

"Then listen. Go to Samuel Clay's house and say this, 'Samuel needs help.' Can you do that?'"

"Yes."

"If you have any trouble getting help, ask for my daughter Star. She knows Cherokee."

A few minutes later, Star showed up with a half-dozen men and a long rope. She called out, "Hang on, Sam! They'll get you out."

Grey stood up and walked over to where Samuel's men were standing. The boy ran over to try to help the men, and Grey heard her tell him in Cherokee that he had done enough to help. The biggest man tied the rope to his waist, and the others braced themselves and began pulling. In a few minutes a sputtering Sam was lying at their feet. Two of the men helped him up, and Star turned to Grey and said, "Wa-do." Then in English, she told Sam, "Let's get you into some dry clothes." Then she repeated the words to the boy in Cherokee.

Before they walked away, Star turned to Grey and said in Cherokee, "Won't you come to the house with us and have some hot stew?"

Star laughed and clapped her hands like the little girl she once was when Grey replied, "Your mother and I will come after I clean up and change clothes."

Blue was all smiles when he told her they were going to Star's house to eat so he clarified matters. "It is just the one time, Blue. I am mainly going because I want to hear how the boy came to be in the water."

She just smiled some more and said, "I understand."

Blue tried to hide her amazement at how much the boy ate. He ate like he hadn't eaten in days, and perhaps he hadn't. After everyone had eaten their fill, including the hired hands, they sat in the kitchen at Star's long wooden table. Grey spoke to the boy, "Tell us what happened."

The boy hesitated, looked over at Grey and asked, "May I say it in Cherokee?"

Grey nodded his approval, and Blue said, "That's all right. Tell us your story, and we will translate for the others."

He bowed his head as if gathering his thoughts and then spoke. "We once lived in the country on a farm, but my mother died when I was small. I barely remember her. When she died, my father was very sad and tried to forget his sorrow by drinking whiskey. For a while, we stayed at the farm, but then the bank took it away because they said my father owed them money he couldn't pay. We moved to town, and my father got a job at the livery stable, and we got a room to stay in and food to eat for his pay. He still drank but only did it at night when he wasn't working. One night about a week ago my father got so drunk that he set the stable on fire and burned it and himself up. I helped the men get the horses out, but the stable owner said I was a no-good like my father, and I would have to leave. I have been walking around ever since then, and I have been camping on your land for the last three nights. This morning I walked down to get me some water to boil some roots to eat when I accidentally fell in and got swept away. If Mister Clay hadn't seen me, I would have drowned."

Then he stood up and said, "Please tell Mister Clay and his men *Wa-do* for the rescue and the food. I will be leaving now to find another place to stay."

Star stood up and said in Cherokee, "No, we want you to stay. We could use the help of a strong smart boy like you."

For the first time Blue saw a smile on the boy's face and hope in his eyes. He said, "I will do my best to earn my keep. Is it all right if I go outside and look around a little?"

Star smiled and patted his arm. "Of course."

Blue came back to see Star the next day and noticed the boy petting Star's big dogs as he fed them She called out, "Hey, boy. What is your name?"

He looked up and grinned at her. "My mother called me Little Bug, but my father shortened it to just Bug or *tsu-s-go-ga*."

When she told Sam about their conversation, he laughed and said, "Ain't that funny? I was just sayin this mornin, 'That boy falls all over hisself to please. He's always junin around.'"

Star walked into the room. "I heard you two talking. I guess 'Junebug' is all right for a nickname, but he needs a real name for school. We could name him after your father, Sam."

Sam raised his bushy red eyebrows. "No boy should be saddled with a name like Mation."

"No, I was thinking about his middle name, David."

"That should work, but don't be disappointed if no one calls him that. Nicknames tend to stick tighter than real ones."

Sam's statement proved prophetic, and the Cherokee orphan became Junebug Clay.

Blue was happy about Star's new addition to her family because she thought caring for the boy might make up for Star's seeming inability to get pregnant. As for Junebug, he proved himself to be willing to work hard at any task he was given, but he excelled with anything related to animals.

One day Sam told June he could have a day off to ride a horse around the countryside. "After all," he told Star, "the boy has worked almost every day since he came to live with us."

Star paused in kneading bread dough long enough to reply. "That's true, but if he would go to school like I want him to, he would have plenty of time to play and friends to play with." Then she went back to kneading dough.

"Don't you remember he tried to go to school to please you, and he hated it?"

"Well, sometimes if we put up with things we think we hate for long enough, we will come to realize it is something we need to do."

Bluebird, who was knitting in the corner of the parlor, had been listening to their conversation. She put her needles down and came into the kitchen where they were. "You're overworking the dough, Star. Your bread will not be as soft as you like it. Not everyone is created to be a scholar like you."

"All right I will stop kneading, but I still think Junebug didn't give school much of a chance."

Bluebird's eyes flashed. "Did he tell you he was made fun of because he can't read? Did he tell you he had to run home every day to keep from getting beaten?"

Star dropped her eyes. "No, he didn't tell me, but if he had, maybe I could have helped him. I know I could teach him to read."

"It was easier for him to say he hated school than to tell you he was the one who was hated."

Sam cleared his throat. "If the boy had talked to me, I could have taught him how to fight."

"It's not too late for you to teach him those things, but don't tell him that I told you his secrets. Now it's time for me to go home and see if I can coax your father into taking a rest."

"Does he still have the bad cough?"

"Yes, and he won't go to the doctor."

"Tell him Star says he better go to the doctor if he doesn't want me to come over and scold him."

"Good idea. I'll try it. "

"You do that. See you in the morning. We will be at your house by eight. We promised to stop by and take the Widow Whitmire along with us so we will need to leave early to keep from being late for church."

"That's fine. I'm always waiting on you anyway."

After supper Star stood on the front porch, looking down the road, hoping to catch a glimpse of Junebug. She heard the door open, and Sam stood beside her. "Still not home?"

"No."

"I better go out and look for him."

Sam saddled up his favorite horse, a sorrel gelding named Rowdy, and had only gone about half a mile when he heard someone speaking Cherokee. "June, is that you?"

"Yes, Mister Sam. I am havin a hard time with this wild horse I found today. The horse you gave me is real steady, and I thought if I could tie them together, I could bring the wild one home. But he keeps spookin and tryin to get away."

"Stay there, and I'll come see if I can help you out."

"All right but come to us slow and easy. There was never a horse as skittish as this one."

Sam got close enough to get a good look at the paint. He was a fine-looking young stallion, with a shiny chestnut and white coat, despite the numerous scratches he had. "Where in the devil did you find him? I ain't seen many like him in these parts."

"He somehow got himself stuck in a thicket over where our property ends and the Christies' begins."

"Well, that explains the scratches and probably why he was there. The Christies do a lot of horse tradin. This one may have strayed from their place. Come on. I'll help you put him in the corral, and we'll ride over to the Christies on Monday and make inquiries."

Junebug's face fell. "Would it be all right if I work with him after church tomorrow?"

"I don't see no harm in that. Now come on. Star's getting worried about you."

SAM COULDN'T TAKE his usual nap during Preacher Scott's overlong sermon because of all the squirming June did that morning. At least the boy was on the receiving end of Star's sharp elbow in the ribs instead of him.

When she scolded June about it on the buggy ride home, he said, "I'm sorry, Miss Star. I'll try to do better next Sunday."

Star patted his cheek. "I know you will. You don't have to call me Miss Star or Sam Mister Star."

"I remember, but is it all right if I call you that?"

Only Sam saw the disappointment in Star's eyes, but she smiled and said, "You can call us whatever you want."

Bluebird tried to smooth things over. "In the old days, Cherokees would sometimes get new names when important events changed their lives. There's no reason why that can't still happen today."

Star smiled gratefully. "Ma, why don't you stay for lunch today? You can fix Pa a plate to take home with you."

"Good idea. He's always glad to eat your cooking."

June inhaled his lunch—as usual—and when Star offered to cut him a piece of apple pie for dessert, he said, "I don't want any right now. Maybe later."

Sam raised his bushy eyebrows. "Can't believe you turned down pie. Guess you're just itchin to work with that paint. Now be careful and holler if you need help. That horse is more than half-wild."

"I will." Junebug jumped up from the table, grabbed his hat, and ran out the back door. Star frowned and shook her head. "Don't you think you better go with him?"

Bluebird spoke up. "No, he shouldn't. Give June room to be a boy."

"I agree with your ma on this one, Star."

"Sometimes I think the two of you conspire against me. Does anybody want pie or not?"

"Have you ever known me to turn down pie?"

"All right. One for Sam. How about you, Ma?"

"I'm going to be like June. Maybe later."

After he finished a big slice of fresh apple pie, Sam watched the boy from the kitchen window. He already had a halter on the paint, and the horse was letting June lead it around like it already belonged to him. It was time to talk to the boy.

Sam walked over to the corral and watched June work the horse. "You're doin real good, June. I'm surprised he's already gentle enough to put up with a halter. Don't overdo it, though. If you try too much too soon, he might balk."

"He's a fast learner. I'm goin to brush him some more and rub him down. Maybe after while I can try him with a blanket."

"Maybe, or you could wait until tomorrow."

"But I have to take him back tomorrow, don't I?"

"We'll see. Give him time to get this lesson soaked in before you teach him anything else."

"All right. Come on, Warrior. Let's get you taken care of."

"Warrior, huh? Don't get too attached. He's not yours yet."

Sam went in to the house to take his usual Sunday afternoon nap. Bluebird grabbed his elbow as he walked into the house. "I have been watching the boy and the horse. Let me go with you to the Christies tomorrow. I can help you with Kate."

"Maybe. I sure would like to figure out some way to buy the horse for the boy, if I can talk Kate Christie into it. People say she ain't your regular housewife. She leaves the cooking and cleaning up to her husband, and she takes care of the finances. She has a reputation for being a tough old gal to bargain with, but I will try my best."

"Well, I have known Kate since the Trail. She was always tough, but her heart is good. We both know that the boy and the horse belong together. We just got to make sure that Kate sees it."

"You can come, but right now I need to take my Sabbath rest."

"I hope that's what Grey is doing, resting. I am going to fix him a plate and go home. Don't forget to come and get me before you go to the Christies."

"I won't forget."

Junebug behaved at supper the same way he did at lunch. He wolfed his food down and hurried outside to continue his training of Warrior. It was nearly dark when Star asked Sam to bring the boy in. The horse was following behind June, as gentle as a lamb, with a blanket sitting securely on his back.

BREAKFAST WAS ANOTHER hurry-up affair. June stood up and said, "I'll go get Warrior ready."

"All right. I'll be right there as soon as I finish my coffee."

Star watched June leave with troubled eyes. "I hope he's not too disappointed."

"Me, too."

Sam caught a glimpse of Bluebird pacing back and forth on the wide front porch before he reigned in his horses in front of her house. June jumped down for a fast check of Warrior, who was tied behind their wagon, and quickly ran to the front of the wagon to assist Bluebird.

Bluebird said, "Let me do the talking," as June helped her climb into the buggy.

The Christie dogs announced their coming when they were half a mile down the road. Kate Christie sat on the front porch, smoking a corncob pipe. She stood up when she recognized her visitors and yelled for the dogs to quiet down.

"Help me down, June, and remember, Sam, let me talk to her in Cherokee first."

"Yes, ma'am."

The two women greeted each other and continued their conversation in Cherokee. All Sam recognized was "hello" and his and June's names. June was listening intently, and someone must have told him to bring the horse over to Katie. She put away her pipe and ran her hands over the young stallion and scowled at the scratches on his back and along his flanks.

From what Sam could tell, both women were bargaining fiercely. From time to time Kate would shake her head, and June's eyes would look worried. Finally, his mother-in-law asked him to speak. "Sam, tell Katie how surprised you were to see what Junebug has already accomplished with the horse."

"Ma'am, I have been around horses all my life, and I ain't never seen a wild horse halter and blanket trained in one day. That's what Junebug did with this paint."

Katie shrugged her shoulders. "Yes, that's pretty good, I have seen it done before, but only once."

"Who did it, ma'am?"

"My son Jess did the same with his first horse in one day. Jess has wanted another one just like that for a long time. He says it was the best horse he ever had, and it was a paint. I arranged to buy this paint and some other horses from a Seminole over in Wewoka. He warned my husband, Dan, that this one is high-spirited and might try to run away. It did, and Dan is out looking for it now. Where did you find it, boy?"

"He was caught in the thicket on the east boundary of our land. It took me a long time to free him and get him to our place."

Kate grinned and slapped June on the shoulder. "I thank you for that, boy, and you deserve a nice reward. What do you think about five silver dollars?"

Sam chuckled. "That's right generous of you, ma'am, but I think my boy would rather have five dollars off of the price of the horse."

Katie raised her eyebrows and looked surprised. "Oh, I didn't know this boy is your son, Mister Clay. I thought he was a Cherokee boy who works for you."

"No, he is my adopted son, and I promised him I would try to buy this horse for him."

"I agree that parents should keep their promises. I made a promise to my son to get him another paint, and that is what I have done. Sorry, this horse is not for sale."

"I would pay you a good price."

"Still not for sale."

Sam looked over at Junebug and saw he was close to tears. Bluebird started bargaining again, but this time she spoke in English. "Kate, we have known each other for a long time, haven't we?"

"Yes, ever since the Trail."

"As an old friend, would you care to make a bet with me?"

"What kind of a bet?"

"If the boy can prove that the horse belongs to him, will you let us buy him for a fair price?"

Kate took her time, lighting her pipe again. Then she turned and faced Bluebird. "What do I get if the boy can't prove it?"

"What do you mean? You get to keep the horse."

"The horse is already mine. I want something extra if you lose."

Sam chuckled to himself. "Ma'am, it's true what they say about you."

Kate's lips formed a sneer. "Not that I care, but what do they say about me?"

"They say you drive a tough bargain."

Kate shrugged her shoulders. "Is that all they say? Of course, I do. I'm in this business to make money, not give it away."

Bluebird walked over to where Kate was standing, stood in front of her, and crossed her arms. "What do you want?"

Kate slowly emptied her pipe and put in fresh tobacco. "What do you offer?"

Sam remembered Kate's reputation for hating to cook. "How about if Bluebird fixes you Sunday dinner for a month?"

"Make that three months, and you have a deal."

Bluebird sputtered, but shook Kate's hand when she offered it.

Sam turned to Junebug. "It's up to you, June."

June patted the paint's neck, touched noses with him, and let go of the reins. He walked over to where Katie was sitting on the porch and whistled. The horse came right to him.

Sam chortled. "Well, there's the proof that the horse belongs to June now."

Kate shook her head. "That's a good trick, but lots of people can whistle a horse to them. I want to see the boy ride him."

Sam's face flushed red. "Ain't that a little much to ask? This horse was just halter and blanket broke yesterday."

"Sorry, that's all I'll settle for."

Bluebird was muttering angrily in Cherokee. Then she motioned June to her and whispered something in his ear. June nodded. Then he walked over to Sam and handed him the reins. They walked into the corral together, and together they placed a blanket on the horse's back. Sam said, "Let him feel your weight first." June spent several minutes leaning on the horse and pushing on his back. Then he whispered something in Warrior's ear.

Junebug climbed up on the corral fence. "Hold him, Mister Sam, while I try."

Sam whispered a prayer as June gently lowered himself onto the horse's back. He handed June the reins. Warrior snorted in shock and laid his ears back. "Uh oh. Hang on, June."

The paint arched his back once in an attempt to dislodge the rider. June locked his arms around the horse's neck and wouldn't budge. He leaned over and whispered in his mount's ear again. Miraculously, the horse relaxed and went into a smooth cantor.

San threw his head back and laughed. "You did it! You did it, June!"

Bluebird turned to Kate and grinned. "Let's talk about a fair price."

"I might settle for a year of Sunday dinners."

"I said a fair price."

"Well, I guess I can find another paint. This one seems to be taken. Two hundred dollars and six months of Sunday dinners."

"Too much. One hundred dollars and a month of Sunday dinners."

"Not enough. One hundred and *fifty* dollars and three months of Sunday dinners."

"How about one hundred and twenty-five dollars, and you come to my daughter Star's house for Sunday dinner for a month."

"Done, if you let me bring my husband and son."

"Done. Sam, pay the woman."

When Sam took Bluebird home, she said, "You and Junebug come in and listen to me tell Grey what we did today. I'll tell it in English, Sam, so you can understand it, too."

Sam had never seen Grey so lively before. When Bluebird told about the bargain she had struck with Kate, he slapped his leg and howled with laughter. He patted Junebug on the back and actually smiled for the first time at his son-in-law. Sam could hardly wait to tell Star what had happened today, but first he had to know the answer to one question. As they walked to their wagon, he asked, "June, what did you whisper in the Paint's ear?"

"I just said, '*e-ree*.'"

"What's that mean?"

"Miss Bluebird said it was Seminole for 'mine.'"

"Well, that makes sense. Speak Seminole to a Seminole horse. Wonder how Bluebird learned Seminole?"

"I don't know, but she is a smart lady. Mister Sam, I want to tell you something.'"

"What's that?"

"Thank you, Pa."

"You're welcome, son."

Grey's attitude toward Samuel Clay changed dramatically that evening. He now accompanied Blue when she visited Star and Sam, and he welcomed both of them into his home. Sam often sent Junebug over to help Grey, and Grey looked forward to his visits. Blue said that Junebug blessed Grey with the opportunity to be a Cherokee grandfather, and he enjoyed teaching his grandson all a Cherokee man should know.

One day, when Blue was gone, Grey was sitting on the front porch when he heard a strange sound coming from the smokehouse. He left the porch and picked up a big stick he found lying on the path to the smokehouse. He might need it if an outlaw was waiting for him inside. He wished he had gone into the house first and got his gun, but he had his hunting knife with him, and maybe the stick and the knife would be enough. Of course, if it was something supernatural, normal weapons wouldn't protect him anyway. Maybe it was some of those little people his mother and grandmother used to leave milk and bread out for. If that was the case, he better speak to them in Cherokee. "Little people, please forgive me for failing to provide you with milk and bread. You are welcome to take all the hog and deer meat that you want from my smokehouse. I promise I will give you plenty of bread and milk tomorrow. Just don't hurt me or my family."

Nothing happened so he quietly crept into the smokehouse. It was dark inside, and he couldn't see what had been making the noise. Then a hand reached out and touched his pants leg, and a voice said, "Help me, Mister. My head hurts so bad, and I am powerful hungry."

Grey ran out of the smokehouse as fast as he could, but he stopped and turned around when he saw a white man emerge from the darkness he had been hiding in. The man staggered into the sunlight, moaned, and fell over.

Grey watched him for a minute, and when the man didn't move, he prodded him with the stick he still carried. The man moaned again, so he wasn't dead. When Grey bent down to examine him more closely, the strong stench of alcohol and vomit almost turned his stomach. What should he do with this stinking white man who had begged him for help? If the white man died, would he get in trouble? He wished Blue were here. She always knew what to do.

He had seen people throw cold water on drunks to wake them up. Maybe he should try that. Grey went to the well, drew a bucket of cold spring water, and threw it all over the man. It worked. The man awoke, sputtering, and cursing.

"Why did you go and do that, mister? I ain't hurtin nobody. All I need is a little food and another bottle of whiskey."

"I will give you a bowl of my wife's chicken and dumplings, but I don't have any whiskey for you."

"Chicken and dumplings sounds good. Is there someplace I can wash off a little before I eat?"

"There is a pump over there. You can use it to clean up. If you want to take off those dirty clothes and leave them, I will leave some of my clean clothes on the porch for you to put on. When you are finished, come into the kitchen, and I will fix you something to eat."

The man looked better after he cleaned up, and ate like a starved dog. "Thanks, mister. I'm sorry if I scared you. My head was splittin because I have had nothing but rot gut whiskey for three days. I don't usually drink like that, but some strangers burned my house down and took all I had. All I have done for three days is wander around, drinkin whiskey. If I could just get me a job, maybe I could get straightened out again. Do you know where I could find work?"

"I might know someone who would hire you. After you finish eating, I will take you to my son-in-law's house."

"Bless you, mister. All I need is a chance."

Grey didn't know why he felt like helping a white man. Maybe it was because he admired what Sam had done for an Indian boy. Or maybe he just wanted the white man off his place. Whatever the reason, he was driving him to Sam's house.

The man offered him his hand. "My name's Andrew Williams. Pleased to meet you."

Grey shook his hand as he had seen white men do. "My name's Grey Wolf. Are you ready to go?"

Blue looked surprised when she saw Grey on the road when she was walking back from visiting Star. He stopped the buggy on the lane and gave her an explanation. "I'm just taking this man over to see Sam. Don't worry about the mess by the pump. I will clean it up."

He drove off before she could ask him any questions. When they got to Sam's house, he told the man, "Wait here," and knocked on the door.

Star answered the door. "Pa, you don't have to knock. Come in."

"I need to talk to Sam about something important. Could you ask him to come out?"

Star looked puzzled, but she said, "Sure. I'll go tell him."

In a few minutes, Sam came out, looking even more puzzled than Star. "What's this all about, Grey?"

Grey gave him a short version of his encounter with Williams. He ended with, "He said he just needed a chance, and he wants to work. I thought maybe you could use him."

Sam sighed. "All right. Tell him to come here. I'll put him up for the night even if I decide not to hire him."

As Grey drove back to his house, he thought about what he had done. For the first time in his life he had helped a white man, and he was glad that he had. He didn't think Blue would mind either, once he had cleaned up the vomit in the smokehouse and thrown away the nasty clothes.

SAM LOOKED AT the wretched man in front of him and listened to his words. After the man had finished his story, Sam said, "I'm going to give you that chance you're asking for, Andrew, but only one. If I see you so much as look at a bottle of whiskey, you're back on the road. Do you understand me?"

"Yes, sir. I do. You won't be sorry you hired me."

"I hope you're right."

Andrew Williams worked for Sam Clay for the next thirty years. He always told anyone who asked him, "If it hadn't been for Sam Clay and his father-in-law, I likely wouldn't be alive today. They gave me the chance I needed."

As he grew older, Grey continued to work, toiling hard on the same land that he and Blue had farmed as sharecroppers and later as owners. He bought twenty more acres that one of his neighbors agreed to sell him, which added to his load. Blue knew how tired Grey was every night when he staggered to bed. He had always had weak lungs, a legacy from the Trail, but recently his condition had worsened. Blue alone heard the way he sometimes shook the bed with his deep, wracking coughs. "You must go to the town doctor and get some medicine, Grey."

"Ha! Why would I trust a white man to give me anything that would help me? I just need to get some strong tea from a medicine man. Is Deer's son still taking care of people?"

"As far as I know, but he is getting to be an old man. Remember, he was a grown man when we were on the Trail."

"Yes, I remember. Well, I will go see him tomorrow morning after I finish hoeing the garden."

The next morning Grey Wolf coughed and hacked when he was washing up for breakfast. He tried to throw the thick mucus away with his wash water, but Blue saw it. "If you don't go see the doctor in town, I am going to ride and get Star. She will make you go."

"All right, you troublesome woman. I will go, so you will give me some peace."

After the examination, Dr. Greene told Blue he needed to speak to her and her husband before they left for home. Blue looked at his face and knew the news was bad.

"Folks, I hate to have to tell you this, but Mister Wolf has pneumonia in both lungs, and he is going to have to stay in bed for some time to recover."

"Stay in bed! I got a farm to take care of."

"If you do any farming in the next few months, your wife will be burying you."

Blue spoke up, "He will do as you say, doctor. Tell me about the medicine I will need to give him."

Grey just said, "Pay him, Blue."

Blue did her best to nurse Grey Wolf, but he was stubborn. When she begged him to rest, Grey would shout, "I got work to do. I can't lie around in bed!"

"Do I need to bring Star over again to talk to you? You need to do what she told you to do. Give Star and Sam our land, so Sam and his hired hands can take care of both farms."

Grey reluctantly agreed, but he still went out every morning to see how the crops were progressing. If Blue didn't keep an eye on him, he would be out hoeing or watering. When he came back from such excursions, he was coughing and completely drained.

Blue awoke to bird songs one early spring morning. Grey was sleeping soundly, and she moved quietly to keep from disturbing him. She propped herself up on her elbow to get a good look at him. His pain-lined face was so thin that his features looked almost hawkish, and the hard muscles in his arms and legs, which she always admired, had almost disappeared. The sickness enemy was winning the war on Grey's body, but she would keep searching for weapons that could stop its onslaught. She had visited every healer and medicine man that she had heard of, but yesterday one of Grey's friends had given him a new name. "You should send someone to talk to Dark Crow for you. He is a medicine man who lives in Nicutt, and everyone says that he is powerful in conjuring medicine. If someone has put this sickness on you by having you conjured, he can break the spell."

"Maybe somebody has conjured me. Blue, do you remember a couple of years ago when we caught those strangers trying to steal some of our hogs? Their old granny told me I would pay for my stinginess. Maybe she was a witch, or maybe someone in the family conjured me. You need to go see this Dark Crow and get the spell broken."

She agreed to go to humor Grey. Today was the day, and she had to get up and get ready.

After creeping quietly from bed, Blue examined her image in the hallway mirror. Worry had made her thinner and older, too. When she pulled back her long dark hair to put it into a bun, she saw the first glints of silver in its roots. It didn't matter. All that mattered was she was strong enough to keep her beloved safe. Blue would gladly visit another medicine man today. This one lived several miles away in Nicutt, but Samuel said that he would take her in his buggy, and Star would spend the day with her father.

BLUE DIDN'T FEEL like talking, so her responses to Samuel's conversational attempts were very short. Finally, the friendly, red-headed giant threw up his hands. "All right, Bluebird, I will leave you in peace. Star always says that I talk too much."

"It is my fault, Samuel. My heart and tongue are both heavy today. I just pray that this new healer can give us hope."

"And so do I. Let's stop, eat a bite, and stretch our legs."

"That's a fine idea. I packed some fried chicken and biscuits for our lunch."

"And Star sent an apple pie for our sweets."

"Star is a good girl and a good cook."

"She is at that. Just like her mama."

"More like Cousin Molly. She taught us how to make pies."

"Well, whoever the teacher was, they did a fine job. Let's pull over in the shade and eat."

Blue got down a chicken wing, a biscuit, and three bites of a slice of pie before she felt full. Samuel, who was happily devouring everything, scolded her. "You got to eat more than that, Bluebird, or you'll get sick like your husband."

"I'm just not very hungry, Samuel. You go ahead and eat all you want. I am going to take care of other needs."

"Oh, all right. Just don't wander too far away. No tellin what kind of varmints live in these woods."

AFTER BLUE RELIEVED herself, she noticed some strange truffles growing a few yards away. She took out her digging knife and began to gather them. A child's voice whispered into her ear, *"Don't you know that you should ask first before taking someone's treasures?"*

Blue threw down the mushrooms and her knife and scrambled to her feet. She looked all around but saw no one. Remembering the stories of her mother, she realized she had trespassed on the property of the *Yunwi Tsundi,* the Cherokee Little People. "Please forgive me. I trespassed in ignorance. Please accept my best digging knife as a gift, and I will not take your mushrooms."

"Why are you here?"

"My son-in-law and I are on our way to visit Dark Crow, the medicine man."

"Why are you visiting him? Do you want to conjure someone?"

"No, I just want to find out if someone has conjured my husband to make him sick. I have heard that Dark Crow can break any conjuring spell."

"Perhaps, but he is better known for making conjuring spells. Dark magic can seldom be turned to white."

Blue nodded in agreement. "But if there is the smallest hope, I have to find it."

"Go ahead, but take the mushrooms with you. They have special medicine in them, and if you boil them in some tea, they will give your mate some relief for a time."

Blue whirled around as she caught a small movement in the corner of her eye. *"Quit trying to peek, or I will take my mushrooms away! I was just picking up the knife."*

"I am sorry. Thank you for the mushrooms."

"I gave them to you because your mother was always kind to my kin. And because I like you, I offer you this advice. Don't trust Dark Crow. Oh, and don't tell anyone that you have seen me. If you do, you will bring trouble on yourself and your family."

"I will heed your advice and warnings. *Wa-do* and I hope to see you again someday."

"Maybe you will, but more likely it will be one of your descendants that will see me."

Bluebird called out, "What do you mean? I only have one daughter." But the being and his voice were gone.

She was startled by the sound of heavy feet walking through the woods. "Bluebird, where are you?"

"I am, here, Samuel."

"You had me worried. Let's get back on the road."

WHEN THEY REACHED the Nicutt settlement, Blue asked Samuel to stop at the first Cherokee home that they came to. "Stay here, Samuel. They won't talk to me if you come with me."

"All right, but holler if you need me."

The cheerful lady of the house turned sour when she asked about Dark Crow. "I can tell you where he lives, but I wouldn't go there if I were you."

"I have to talk to him."

After several twists and turns, Blue and Samuel found a small, dark house, almost hidden behind tall cedars. "I better go with you this time."

"No, you have to stay here."

As Blue raised her fist to knock on the door, it opened, and she looked into the face of an impassive Cherokee elder. "I have been waiting for you, daughter."

"I am honored to meet you, healer."

"A few have called me healer, but most call me Dark Crow. Why do you seek me out?"

"My husband is very sick, and I thought someone may have conjured him to cause the sickness."

Dark Crow scowled. "What is that to me? I have not conjured him."

"I have heard that you can break conjuring spells."

"Yes, sometimes, for a price."

"How much?"

"How much do you have?"

"Twenty dollars in silver."

"Give it to me, and I will see what I can do. Go sit on the porch, and I will smoke on it. When I am finished, I will come out and talk to you."

The wait was long, and Blue feared that Samuel would soon start yelling for her to come back. Finally, Dark Crow came out of his house. "The spell is broken, and you can leave now."

"Will my husband get well now?"

"I cannot say since I am not a healer. You paid me to break a conjuring spell, and that is what I have done. Now, be gone." He slammed the door and went back into his dark house.

She shook Samuel's shoulder to wake him up. He stared from bleary blue eyes. "You don't look happy. Wouldn't he help you?"

"He helped himself to my money. I don't know if he did anything for Grey."

"Well, maybe telling Grey you visited the medicine man will be enough."

Blue smiled. "Now I know why my daughter married you."

"What do you mean by that?"

"You are a very wise man."

Samuel shook his head. "Now I know you're joshin me. Star's always been the smart one. I ain't smart at all."

"Yes, you are. Grey will feel better because he will no longer be afraid he has been conjured. This trip will help my husband."

"Hmmm... maybe I'm not so dumb, after all."

SAMUEL WAS RIGHT. Grey's eyes lit up when Blue told him that she had visited Dark Crow, and he said he had broken the conjuring spell. The mushroom medicine somehow calmed the deep coughs, and Grey was hungry again. He said, "I am well," and Blue smiled and believed him.

Less than a year later, the sickness came back. Despite all kinds of medicine, White and Cherokee, Grey was not recovering. Near the end, he mostly slept. One unusually warm October morning, he asked Sam if he would carry him to the back porch. He sat on the back porch all morning, looking at the foliage and telling Star stories about his days in North Carolina and their early days in Indian Territory. His last words to her were, "You know I have done some dark things in my life that only your mother knows. Maybe someday she will see fit to tell you. But one thing I want you to know. I am a happy man, and I have made my peace with Creator. I have even come to love this new place as much as my home in the old land. Now you go on home and fix your husband some supper. He's a good man for a white man."

"No, Father, I want to stay with you. Samuel can take care of himself."

"You go on, now. I'm just going to take a little nap, here in the sunshine. It may not be so pretty tomorrow."

Star gave him a hug and walked through the house. "He told me to go home," she told her mother.

"Go on then. Ask Samuel if he will come over after supper and help me get your father back in bed."

Star had barely settled in the wagon when she heard her mother's cries. Grey Wolf, survivor of the Trail of Tears, her father, had passed away in his early forties.

Star hurried to her mother's side and joined her in the rocking, keening lament that seems universal to grieving women everywhere. Later she would realize that the Cherokee she thought she had forgotten had somehow, in the trauma she experienced, been restored to full use.

Star felt Sam's hand on her shoulder and sensed the great width and the depth of the love he held for her. The three of them knelt over Grey Wolf's body for some time until finally her mother raised up, with tears streaming, and asked, "How shall I live without him?"

"I will help you, Mother."

"And so will I, Mother Bluebird. You are welcome to make your home with us."

Bluebird embraced Star and patted Sam's arm. "Thank you, children. Now, we have things to do. Sam, please go to Katie Springwater's house and ask her if she can come over and help us with Grey Wolf's body. You can also ask her to send her husband to tell Pathseeker what has happened."

She stopped speaking and turned to Star. "What am I forgetting?"

"Stop by the church and tell Pastor Scott, Sam."

"Wa-do, daughter. But, Sam, tell the preacher to wait until tomorrow to come and see us. I want to talk to Pathseeker first. Let me know if there is anything else I have forgotten. Would you mind staying with me while Sam runs the errands?"

"Not at all."

It wasn't long until Katie and the midwife Kohene came to help with laying out the body. By the time, Pathseeker and two other elders arrived, the hard task was finished, and Bluebird and Star had prepared themselves for company. Pathseeker took their hands and said, "I am sorry you have lost the man of your hearth. I will be glad to arrange what is necessary for the wake and the burial ceremony."

Bluebird bowed her head in agreement. "Wa-do. I was just a child when I attended my father's wake, and I need and appreciate your help very much."

Star asked, "Won't we have a regular funeral for Pa in our church?"

Pathseeker smiled at her. "Of course, you can have a white funeral for your father, but first we must follow the Cherokee tradition of sitting up with the body during a wake. We will help you move the body somewhere where all may see it. Then we will stay and pray throughout the night and get word to others to bring food and help sit with the body tomorrow and tomorrow night. Then a funeral may be held, and the body buried. By that time, Grey Wolf's soul should have finished his travels and be ready to rest."

"Ma, is this what you want?"

"Yes, and more importantly, this is what your father wanted."

Star kept her peace and allowed Pathseeker and the other elders to have their way. The next day many of her parents' stomp dance friends came and brought food. As she was handing Star a large pot of chicken and dumplings, a plump, smiling older woman said, "Are you Star? It's been so long since I saw you and you're all-grown up now, but I thought I recognized you."

"Yes, I'm Star. You're Missus Muskrat, right? I remember eating your chicken and dumplings when I was little."

"Oh, you remember my dumplings, aye? They should be good. I have been makin them for over forty years."

Star met many others like Mrs. Muskrat who shared their best dishes and warm memories with her mother. Several traveled for a number of miles to pay their respects to her father and offer support to Bluebird and Star. Some brought their bedrolls and slept by a big fire that was kept burning the two nights that her father's body stayed at home.

On the morning of the third day, the undertaker came driving a carriage hearse that contained a coffin. Everyone left the house while he prepared the body for burial. Some waved goodbye as they returned to their homes. Others followed Bluebird, Star, Junebug, and Sam as they followed in their own buggy. Star wiped her own tears and put her arm around June as he cried and sniffled. Sam took his right hand off of the reins and patted Star's hand. Only Bluebird was dry-eyed, but her bottom lip quivered, and she put her hand up to her mouth to stop its movement.

After it was all over, and her father was buried under his favorite tree, Star pulled her mother aside from the other mourners. "Ma, I tried to respect Pa's last wishes, but I hope you just ask for a regular funeral."

"It seemed right to me, and I liked having my friends around me."

"Yes, I am glad you had friends to help you. It's not that I didn't like what was done. I just don't think I would know what to do if you asked me to arrange a Cherokee wake."

Bluebird smiled and patted her cheek. "Let's hope I don't have to make that decision for a very long time. Can you come over tomorrow and help me pack the things I want to bring to your house?"

"Of course."

IV
STAR

SOMETHING WAS BOTHERING Sam, but he never said anything. That in itself was a clue he was worried because he was normally a cheerful, talkative man. Her mother offered her counsel. "Leave him alone. He will tell you in his own time."

Junebug would just say, "Pa will talk when he's got somethin to say."

One morning Sam said, "Bring your coffee and sit with me on the porch. We need to talk."

Star felt a sudden flutter of fear in the pit of her stomach, but she remained silent. She suspected he was going to talk about war again, a subject she detested. Star slowly sipped her coffee while she peered over the cup, studying her husband's troubled face.

"Well, I might as well tell you. But promise me you won't cry."

"I can't promise anything until I have your news."

"All right. I joined up yesterday, and I will be leavin here next week."

She slammed her coffee cup down. "Why?"

"Oh, for any number of reasons. For one, there's the hundred dollars that Paul Stanford is offering any local man who will sign with the Union before the end of the year. That money will help carry us through if we have another bad year."

"We've been making it fine, and I don't see why that will change. How about Ma and me? What are we supposed to do when you're off playing soldier? How can two women and two hands plant the crops, work the fields, bring in the harvest? Without you, we will all starve!"

"Now, Star. I'm sorry that most of our hands have quit us to go to war, but the truth is we can't afford to pay as many men as we once did anyway. You know that I would never leave you if there was any danger of that. I have already hired Ed Briggs' son to oversee the place. He needs the work, and he's a good man. His name is Jim. He will see to it that everything is done right. Junebug is practically a man now, and Henry and Andrew are good help, too."

"You know why this Jim needs work, don't you? Because the blamed war took his arm off! And it could do the same to you!" Star shook with anger as all of her resentment and arguments against the war came out in one forceful gush. "What if you come back from the war without your arms or legs, or what if you don't come back at all? I lost my father just a year ago. So, now, I am going to lose you, too? I can't live without you! No, you can't go! Tell that rich Stanford man that you have changed your mind."

Sam rose to his feet and attempted to take Star in his arms, but she pushed him away. "Now settle down, Star. This war is almost over. Our boys have the Rebs on the run. Everyone says that it can't go on more than another year at the outside, and I'll be back before you have time to miss me."

"Oh, what do you know, you stupid, stubborn man! Why don't you tell me the real reason you want to go off and get yourself killed?"

"All right, besides money, I don't hold with the idea of the Confederates holdin theirselves above the law. Who are they to leave the Union, just because they can't get their way? And, I know you feel the same way that I do about slavery. It just ain't right for them to own people and treat them like they're stock! I'm fightin for what I believe in, and if I have to get hurt or die for that, then so be it!"

"That's all big talk, but those aren't the only reasons that you are going to war."

"Is that so? And what other reason could I have?"

"You're doing it out of pride. For the last year, I have seen how you hang your head every time you attend one of those war rallies, and old men like Stanford get up and brag on the brave men who are off fighting for their country. You foolishly think you are less than a man because you stay home and take care of your place. Isn't that right?"

Sam bellowed. "All right, woman! Have it your way. Yes, there are some who have called me a coward behind my back, and rightfully so! Do you realize I am one of a very small number of able-bodied men livin hereabouts that hasn't volunteered to do his duty? Yes, that's part of why I'm goin off to fight, but those other reasons I gave are just as valid. So, whatever you say, and however much you cry, I will be ridin out a week from today. Now come and kiss me and give me good memories of my lovin wife to carry me through."

"Kiss yourself! I don't want to have anything to do with such a fool!"

Star kept to her word for the rest of the day, and in the evening, she moved her quilt and pillow into a spare room. Bluebird saw her there. "Why are you not sleeping with your husband tonight, Star?"

"My husband is leaving me to fight a war."

Bluebird sighed deeply and then sat beside her on the bed. "That is a hard thing. When is he leaving?"

"Next week."

"Such a short time! What are you doing here when you need to spend that short time with the one that you love?"

"You don't understand! I can't stand the thought of losing him!"

"And you don't understand. You are losing him now because you won't spend time with him. Star, men have always left women, but if they can at all, they come back to those women who hold them tight and show them they are loved. When Sam is fearful or hurt, who do you think he will see? It will be the picture of you in his arms that will calm his fears, heal his wounds, and bring him back to your side."

Star carried her quilt and pillow back to her marriage bed. Sam smiled when he saw her, opened wide his arms, and embraced her with abundant enthusiasm.

SEVERAL MONTHS LATER, Star groaned as she pulled her exhausted body from the sweat-drenched sheets of her bed. Lord, it is barely daylight and already burning hot!

She heard her mother singing in Cherokee in the kitchen as she fried bacon and eggs for the household. She saw Star and switched to English. "Good morning, Star. Come and have breakfast with us."

"I'll eat later, Ma. I need to go check on the crops. Jim, you need to hurry up, eat, and come join me in a few minutes."

"Sure will, Missus Clay. I will be right there."

Then he turned to Henry, Andrew, and Junebug. "Better hurry up and eat, boys! The boss is on the move."

Star looked at the rows of green beans, squash, peas, onions, lettuce, tomatoes, and radishes. They were all thriving as were the carrots, cucumbers, cabbages, and potatoes, but the weeds were creeping in. Jim joined her on her walk to the corn field. She shucked an ear and frowned.

"Jim, look at the color of the leaves! They barely have any green to them. You're going to have to water this corn more often. The sun is about to burn it up."

"I know, Missus Clay, but all of us have been so busy tryin to save the beans, peas, squash, and everything else that we had to let something go, and guess that was the corn. We'll water it before the day is up."

"We can't afford to let anything go, Jim. Times are hard, and we need everything we grow to do well if we are going to have anything extra to sell this year. We have to sell, or we can't pay the bank what we owe them for the loan they gave us. And if we don't pay the bank, they will take everything. You don't want that to happen, do you?"

"No, Ma'am, but as you seen for yourself, we got a lot of weedin and hoein to do."

"All right. Just don't neglect watering the corn."

"We won't."

Star soon busied herself, feeding and watering all of the animals that lived on the farm. Jim stopped her when he saw her carrying two heavy buckets full of slop to the hog pens. "Missus Clay, let me do that for you. Them buckets is too heavy for a woman."

"I thought you were working in the fields."

"I was but stopped long enough to get some water for me and the boys. It's mighty hot today!"

"It is that. All right, you can have these buckets. Are you sure you can manage them with just one arm?"

The wiry short man sputtered. "Just give them to me, Ma'am. I am stronger with my good arm than a lot of men are with their two."

"Yes, I suppose you are. After you finish with the hogs, you better all take a water break. I don't want anyone passing out from the heat. I'll just go tend to the chickens."

"Yes, Ma'am. Don't forget to get yourself some water and something to eat."

"Sure. I'll take a break soon."

But she forgot until Bluebird tapped her on the shoulder as she was gathering eggs in the hen house. Star gasped. "Ma, you scared me! I thought I was the only one in here."

"You need to come in the house and eat and drink something before you faint."

"All right if you insist, but I have a lot to do."

"So do we all. But we must take care of ourselves first."

Star took a drink from the dipper in the kitchen, grabbed herself a slice of bacon, which she put in a biscuit. As she started to open the kitchen door, her mother grabbed her arm. "No, sit down and rest a bit first."

"I really don't have time, Ma."

"Star, you must take time to take care of yourself. You are losing weight, you are barely sleeping, and you don't look healthy."

"I am fine. Quit worrying."

At the midday meal of fresh ham, gravy, fresh tomatoes, and leftover biscuits, Star asked Jim, "Have you watered the corn yet?"

"No, haven't gotten around to it yet."

At the evening meal, Star asked again, "Did you water the corn today, by chance?"

"No, sorry. It took the whole day just to tend to the weedin and hoein. On top of that, we had to mend fence where the critters have been gettin in. We'll water the corn first thing in the mornin."

"Never mind then. I'll water the corn myself."

"Are you sure, Missus Clay? That's a lot of waterin for a woman to do. Sure it can't wait till mornin?"

"No, it can't wait."

Junebug spoke up. "Let me help you, Ma."

"Did you remember to water all of the stock tonight—not just the horses?"

June wouldn't look at her. "I kinda forgot about the mules."

"Remember what I said about how important it is to give the animals extra water when it's hot like it has been?"

"I remember. I just don't work with the mules much."

"Well, take care of them, and then you may come help me."

"All right."

Bluebird was washing the supper dishes when she looked out the kitchen window and saw her daughter walking to the well house with two buckets in her hands. She dried her hands and quickly walked outside. "Star, you shouldn't water now."

"Why?"

"In the evening time the snakes come out, looking for water and a cool place to lie."

"Ma, we haven't seen a snake around here in years. I will be fine."

"You should listen to me, but if you won't, take the dogs with you."

"Oh, all right. Come on, boys."

Star gave a shrill whistle, and two hounds, one elderly and one young, ran eagerly to her side. "Hey, Bear! Hey, Ox! How are you boys doing? You want to go to the well house with me?"

The dogs wagged their tails and licked her hands when she scratched behind their ears. "Good boys. Come on then."

Bluebird stayed in the yard, peering anxiously after her daughter's retreating figure. A few minutes later, she heard Star scream, Bear yelp, and Ox bark fiercely. Something was wrong! Forgetting her age, she grabbed a nearby hoe and ran to the well house.

When she got there, her quick mind saw what had happened. A large copperhead was coiled up a few inches from where Star was standing. Both dogs were standing in front of Star, and both were growling and snapping at the snake. The snake's attention was on the dogs and Star, and it didn't sense that its death was in the hands of the small Indian woman. Bluebird brought the edge of the hoe down on the head of the serpent, neatly decapitating it with one blow. Star exhaled nosily. "Thanks, Ma! I'm glad you came. I was afraid to move in case it struck at me or at the dogs again. It got poor Bear, but he's still fighting. Such a good boy!"

Star patted and hugged Bear. "Can you save him, Ma?"

"I will try, but I may not have time. His leg is already swelling. Get one of your men to carry him into the house."

Junebug came running to the well house. "I heard screaming. What happened?"

"Poor Bear got snake bit, trying to save me. Would you carry him in to the storeroom?"

June put his arms under the dog and gently lifted him up. His bottom lip quivered. "Is he goin to be all right?"

Star gave him a quick hug. "We hope so."

Star turned to her mother. "All right. Next time I will listen to you, Ma. No more watering at dusk."

"That's good. Now let's see about this brave Bear dog."

LATER THAT NIGHT, after she had tried every remedy she could think of, Bluebird sighed. "Oh, Bear, poor boy. I couldn't save your namesake, and I can't save you. Let me get your mistress so she can say goodbye to you."

Bluebird walked to Star's bedroom where Star sat, napping in a chair. "Star, he's going. You will want to tell him goodbye."

Star cried out. "Oh, not my Bear dog! Sam gave him to me when we were just kids. Remember you said he reminded you of the dog you had when you were young? That's why I named him Bear."

"He doesn't look much like my Bear, except for being big, but he has Bear's brave heart."

Star wiped her streaming eyes and took her mother's offered hand. "Is he in pain, Ma?"

"No, I gave him something to put him to sleep. But you need to come now."

Star stumbled to where Bear was lying on a cot in the spare room. "Hello, Bear." She began crying again when she saw a slow movement under the quilt covering her dog.

"Ma, after all that he's been through, he's still trying to wag his tail." She stretched out her hand and scratched behind his ears.

"What a brave, brave dog you are, Bear! There has never been another dog as brave and good as you."

"Yes, he is just like my Bear. My Bear died trying to defend me from the white soldiers, and your Bear died defending you from the copperhead. Now send him off to the good place where good dogs go."

"I will. Just let me just sit here by myself for a while, all right?"

"Sit as long as you want. I am going to get ready for bed."

Star sobbed as she stroked her beloved dog's head and neck. His great heart soon quit beating. "Goodbye, Bear Dog. We will meet again someday, somewhere beyond the stars."

Star wiped her eyes as she looked up at her namesakes as they appeared over the horizon. I wonder where Sam is tonight. Is he looking at the stars like me? I hope he's somewhere safe, sound asleep. I need to go to sleep myself, but I am just so tired. Can you be too tired to sleep? That's how I feel right now. Lord, I can't do this by myself much longer! It's been over a year now. Please, send Sam home to me, soon.

Bluebird was brushing her long black hair when Star came into her room, wiping away the last of her tears. "He's gone, Ma. I'm going to miss him."

"Yes, you will, but you will see him again someday."

"Do you really believe that?"

"Yes, I do. Just like I will see your father someday, and my mother, and my own Bear dog."

"Good night, Ma."

"Good night, dear one."

Despite her fatigue, Star lay awake for some time mourning her dog and worrying about her husband.

STAR SAT ON the front porch, munching on a biscuit spread with fresh butter and strawberry jam, sipping dark coffee, made lighter with fresh cream. Everyone was telling her to rest more, even Jim. "Missus Clay, when your husband left me in charge some two years ago, he told me to take care of the place and to watch after you. Well, I hate to say it, but I ain't done such a good job of watchin after you. If you don't stop now and then and rest and eat, you are just goin to dry up and blow away."

To get a little peace, she had agreed to sit on the front porch every morning, eating a little breakfast before she started her busy day. She also agreed to sit down and eat more at the midday and evening meals.

Jim looked worried when he came up on the porch. Star tried to guess what bad news he was bringing her.

"Ma'am, Henry left us last night. His father sent one of his slaves over to our sleepin quarters to fetch him home."

"I didn't know Henry's parents have slaves."

"Just two or three which have been with the family a long time. Anyway, before he left he said his family was goin to Texas, and they wanted him to go along. He said to tell you he was sure sorry, but he had to obey his pa."

"But, why are they going to Texas, Jim?"

"Oh, didn't you know? Them pin soldiers are threatenin all the Confederates that live around here. They're tellin em if they don't join the Union, their boys will be shot."

"That's terrible. I hate that our side is resorting to such tactics."

"Well, at least Henry's family is Cherokees, and they got a place to go. I heard tell there's a big bunch of Cherokees and Choctaws campin close to the Red River, and I believe I heard there's some Creeks and other kinds of Indians with them. That's where Henry and his folks will be goin."

"Well, I just hope they're safe in Texas."

"Safer there than here, Ma'am. Sure do hate to lose Henry, though. He was a good hand."

"I'll try to help take up the slack."

"Don't even think about it. I'll ask around. There's plenty of men lookin for work around here. Andrew, Junebug, and me will just work a little harder till I hire somebody."

Andrew came to her the next morning and tried to hand her two pay envelopes. "I don't need these, Miss Star. What do I need money for? I ain't married, and I got a good place to sleep and all the food I want to eat. Mister Sam he even gave me a horse to take me where I want to go. Here, use this money to buy somethin you need like grain for the stock or such."

"Andrew, I wouldn't feel right about taking your money."

"Well, I'm not takin it back."

"In that case I will put it in the wall safe and save it for you. Someday you may need money to get married or put down on a place."

Andrew grinned. "Suit yourself, but I ain't really interested in stuff like that."

"Well, I'll keep it for you, anyway. In case you change your mind."

Despite his optimism, though, Jim didn't find a replacement for Henry right away. He stood on the porch, in front of Star, staring down into his hat. "A lot of folks don't want their husbands, sons, or whoever to stay way out in the country like this is, you know. There's so much meanness goin on right now that folks are afraid somethin bad will happen to em. Just like what happened over at Henry's house."

"What happened?"

"Somebody came in after the family left and burned the house, the barn, and the out buildings down to the ground. Anyway, ma'am, guess that's why I can't replace Henry."

Star looked at the dejected little man, who was avoiding looking her in the face, and plastered on a smile. "That's all right, Jim. I know you tried your best to find another hand, and I don't blame folks for being fearful. What does your wife think about your staying out here with my mother and me?"

Jim snickered. "She don't care, ma'am. She reckons I'm like an old stray tomcat 'cause I always land on my feet. When I was born, the midwife gave me up. Said I was as yeller as a punkin and as dried-up as a prune, but I proved her wrong. My wife was the purtiest gal around, and all my friends told me to quit tryin to court her 'cause I didn't have a chance with her. But she chose me over a lot of better lookin, smoother talkin fellers. And you know the Rebs left me layin in a ditch for dead when I was in the war. But I fooled em and lived, even if I did lose an arm to infection."

Star chuckled. "It sounds like you might be a lucky man to keep around the house."

Jim grinned. "Well, maybe I am, at that."

THAT NIGHT, STAR carried out her nightly ritual of looking at the stars as she sat on the front porch and thought about Sam. Maybe it was all the talk of violence, but something had stolen the sense of peace her nightly ritual always gave her. She was uneasy in her spirit, and she started at every sound. Hearing Ox growl, she ran into the house and locked the front door.

Her mother met her in the hallway. In her hands she carried a coal oil lamp. "What's Ox growling at?"

"I don't know, but we better be prepared in case there's trouble."

About that time, they heard Ox yelp as if kicked or struck. Star grimaced and said, "We better get the guns."

Star jumped as Junebug put his hand on her arm. "Lord, you scared me to death!"

"Sorry, Ma. Is something wrong? Can I help?"

"Here, take this pistol and go back into your room. If anyone besides us tries to come in, shoot them."

Junebug hugged her and took the gun. "Holler if you need me, all right?"

"I will. Now go."

A few minutes later someone banged on the front door. Her mother put her hand on Star's shoulder. "Don't answer that. It's not Jim or Andrew. They always use the back door."

"What if it's Sam?"

"Sam would be yelling at the top of his lungs. Don't answer it."

A few minutes later the wooden door fell with a crash, along with the log the three intruders used to bring it down. Bluebird hissed, "Quick, Star, hide under the bed! Let me do the talking."

Star didn't like it, but she obeyed her mother. As soon as Bluebird left the bedroom, she sprang from the bed and hid behind the door where she could watch what was happening. She saw her mother take the coal oil lamp and walk into the living room where the men rifled through their belongings. Bluebird assumed a humble demeanor. "Is there anything I can help you gentlemen find?"

The leader scowled at her and spat a wad of brown tobacco juice at her feet. "Well, squaw, you can tell us where the folks that live here is."

"The husband is fighting in the war, and the wife is away, visiting her sister. I am the only one here now."

In three strides, the huge bearded man stood in front of Blue. He grabbed a handful of her long hair and twisted it. Star swallowed a gasp, but her mother remained unmoved.

"You make sure you're tellin me the truth, squaw, or you will pay for your lies."

Bluebird kept her eyes lowered. "I am telling the truth. I am the only one here."

He dropped the hair and grinned, showing his tobacco-stained yellow teeth. "All right, then. Show me where they keep their money."

"They didn't leave any money here."

Another man, shorter and slimmer than the leader, took out a hunting knife. "She's lyin. Let me cut her. I'll get the truth out of her."

Bluebird held out her hand as if the stop him. "There's no money in this room, but there's money hid in other places."

"Put the knife away, Brogan. The squaw here is goin to show us where the money is hid."

Star heard her mother say, "We have to go through the kitchen."

Then she couldn't see or hear her mother anymore. Star closed her eyes and said a quick prayer. She rummaged under the bed until she found the shot gun Sam kept there. Now she just had to be quiet and follow behind the third man, who brought up the rear. She would wait for her chance to use the gun.

Her mother shone the light around the kitchen. "Missus Clay keeps money in a sugar bowl she keeps in a kitchen cabinet. I can't reach it without getting something to climb on."

"That's all right. I can reach it. Which one is it?"

"The top one. It's on the far right."

"Come here, Slim. Hand me the torch so I can see somethin. That lamp don't put out much light."

Star watched as the third man moved to the leader's side. Good. Now there was less chance of them seeing her, hiding by the heavy kitchen hutch.

In a few minutes the big man located the sugar bowl and lowered it to the table's surface. He upturned it, and several coins rolled out. He snarled. "Bah! Not much here. A little silver and change."

He turned his attention back to Blue. "There better be more than this, squaw, or I'll let Brogan have his turn at you.'

"There's more, but it's hid on the back porch. Let me unlock the back door, and I will show you where it is."

Bluebird threw back the bar that locked the door, set her lamp on the porch, and quickly threw herself off into the bushes. The leader cursed and said, "Don't let the squaw get away, Slim. Take the torch and go after her. Shoot her when you find her. Me and Brogan will look around the place for valuables."

The two men emptied the potted plants that sat on the back porch and looked through a pile of tools the hands had left there. They stopped when a gun shot rang out. "Well, sounds like Slim plugged the squaw. Come on, Brogan."

Star heard them walk through the back door. Star fought back tears as she got to her feet and raised the shotgun to her shoulder. She prepared to fire.

She never had to shoot the gun because Jim and Andrew burst through the back door, with pistols blazing. The two outlaws fell at her feet. "Thank, God, Jim! "

She put down the shotgun, and she sat down heavily in one of the table chairs as her legs gave way. "Go find Ma, Jim. There's one more man, and he shot her." Then she put her head on the table and cried.

Jim ran over and patted her hand. "Now, now, Ma'am. Don't cry. Your ma is fine. See, she's comin through the back door right now, along with Junebug."

Bluebird came over and sat beside Star. "It's all right, Star. Before I threw myself over the porch, I set the light down on the porch. I saw Jim and Andrew hiding nearby. I figured they could see well enough by the light of the lamp."

Star sat up and looked at her mother. "How about the gunshot?"

"That was me, shootin at the man who was after Grandma Bluebird." Junebug pulled himself to his full height and grinned broadly.

"I thought I told you to stay in the bedroom."

"I did stay there for a few minutes, but then I heard them men yellin at Grandma, and I knew I had to do somethin. I slipped out the front door and got to the back in time to see that man chase after her. Well, I think I winged him, but he ran off before I could catch him. Thought I better check on Granny."

"I don't like you disobeying me, but I'm glad you were there. And seeing about your grandma was more important than running down a bad man."

"That's all right, Ma. Glad to do it."

Jim knelt beside the big man. "This one's still alive. He ain't worth it, but I guess we better try to save his worthless hide. Here, Andrew, help me carry him to the store room. We'll doctor him the best we can, and then I'll put a lock on the storehouse. We'll load him in the wagon and take him to Fort Gibson as soon as it's daylight. They got a doctor over there and men to guard him and decide what should be done with him. We'll bury the one with the knife when we get back."

"How about the one who got away?"

Jim turned a worried face to Star. "He's likely miles away from here by now. But, just to be safe, keep Sam's gun close to hand. Sure wish Henry was here to stay with you. Maybe I better leave Andrew behind."

"No, you take Andrew with you. You'll want him to ride in the back with your prisoner just in case he wakes up."

Junebug spoke up. "Don't worry, Jim. I'll watch over them."

Jim had taken his hat off and was staring into it. Bluebird interrupted his revery. "While you think, I'm going to get ready for bed."

Jim didn't seem to hear her. Finally, he put his hat on his head and faced Star. "I suppose you're right, but I sure hate to leave two women and a boy alone with an outlaw on the loose."

"We'll be fine. Just get some rest, take him to Fort Gibson, and hurry back."

"We will. But, promise me, all of you will be careful and keep your eyes peeled."

Junebug raised his right hand. "I promise."

Early the next morning Bluebird handed Jim and Andrew each a cup of coffee and a biscuit with ham in it. "On the table is a basket full of biscuits with cold ham. Take it with you. I'll feed you better when you get home."

"Thanks, ma'am. Biscuits with ham will do us fine."

Star watched the men until they got out of sight. "Ma, I need to see about Ox. He's whining under the back porch, and he might be hurt bad."

"Don't be too long about it. You need your breakfast. And take Sam's shotgun with you."

"All right, if you insist."

June picked up the gun he had laid on the kitchen table. "I'm goin, too, Ma, and I'll bring my pistol."

Star raised her eyebrows. "Your gun?"

"Why not? I know how to use it."

"Go ahead and bring it. We'll talk about it later."

She walked to the back porch and whistled for her dog. "Hey, Ox! Come here, boy."

She heard Ox get up, and in a few minutes, he appeared at her feet, wagging his tail. Star scratched behind his ears and under his chin. "Are you okay? Let me see if those bad men hurt you." Star ran her hands over the big, red-bone hound's body. He yelped when she touched his right flank.

Star winced and rubbed the dog's ears. "Oh, sorry, Ox. That must be where they kicked him. Nothing's broken, but he may be a little sore and stiff for a while. Are you hungry, boy?"

Ox barked and resumed wagging his tail. "I think that means yes, Ma." June patted the dog's big head, and he licked his face.

"I think you're right. Go in the house and get him some table scraps. Grab yourself a biscuit while you're in there."

June hurried away. Suddenly Ox raised his head and sniffed the air. He barked and looked at her as if wanting her to follow him. Walking quietly and carefully, she carried the shotgun with her as she followed Ox into the woods. As she followed, she looked down at the ground and noticed she was following a blood trail. He barked once more and stopped at the foot of a tall oak tree.

She heard a rustling in the leaves and whirled around. The outlaw yanked the shotgun out of her arms and knocked her down. All she could see was his malicious grin as he lowered the gunstock toward her head.

Then a gun shot rang out, and the missing outlaw crumpled at her feet. "I aimed for the head like Grandpa Wolf told me. He said he hoped I never had to shoot anybody, but if I had to, I should aim at the head."

Junebug was still aiming the pistol at the spot where the outlaw had been standing. Star gently put her hand on the gun and took it away from him. She put her arm around June and hugged him. "Your grandpa would have been happy that his lesson saved my life."

She walked back to the house and saw Bluebird nodding in her rocking chair. She gently shook her shoulder. "Ma, we found the one June shot. He's lying dead in the woods. We can all rest easy now."

Early the next morning, when he finally calmed down after hearing her news, Star told Jim to sit down and eat. "Sometime today you and Andrew can bury both of the bodies in one big hole if you want to."

Jim sat down, but he didn't eat. "I'm still worried, ma'am. I told the Commander that one of the bad men got away. Now I'm goin to have to tell them that we killed him, too."

Junebug 's face looked twisted by his efforts to keep from crying. "If they find out an Indian like me killed him, they will hang me."

Star took him in her arms. "No one would blame a boy for saving his mother's life."

Bluebird scoffed. "Why say anything? For all they know he did get away. They won't care as long as they have the leader."

Jim pursed his lips and chewed on his moustache. "It still don't seem right."

Star shrugged her shoulders. "I think Ma is right. Why stir up trouble for ourselves, especially for June? Now, let's eat. These last two days have been long and hard, and for once, I'm hungry."

Jim nodded his head. "You're the boss. Now pass me some of them taters."

BLUEBIRD WAS AT the cook stove, stirring a pot of stew

when she heard a loud banging at the kitchen door. Jim rushed to answer it. She stopped what she was doing and went to the front porch. "Star, someone is at the back door."

About that time Jim ran to where Star was sitting. "Sorry, Ma'am, but I can't wait to share the good news. One of the Christies' hired hands brought over this newspaper for us to read. The war ended last month, and our side won!"

Bluebird grinned, and her eyes twinkled. "That is good news, Jim. You can tell Star and June all about it while I get back to my stew. I can't let it burn."

Star laughed and cried at the same time. "Did you really say that the war was over, Jim? That is wonderful news! It's been almost three years, but now Sam will finally come home."

June whooped. "Pa's comin home!"

"That's for sure, although it may take a while for some of them soldiers to get home. Do you have any idea where Sam is at?"

"Last I heard, his regiment was fighting in Kansas."

"Well, sir, Grant and Lee made peace at Appomattox Courthouse in Virginia. That's what this paper says."

"May I see that?" Star quickly scanned the front page. "Yes, you're right, Jim. Thank God! The war is really over, and Sam is on his way home."

A few days later, Bluebird was looking out the window when she saw Junebug riding up in a cloud of dust. He came running into the kitchen, shouting in Cherokee.

Star was tired from working in the fields all day and disappointed that Sam still hadn't come home. Junebug's loud impulsive behavior annoyed her. "June, what do you mean running in here, being all loud, and yelling in Cherokee? Nobody can understand what you are saying."

Bluebird came into the room. "I can understand him. He said Henry Bighorse is coming home from Texas."

Star sighed and said, "I'm sorry, Junebug. Go wash up and tell us your news while we eat."

"I'm sorry, too, Ma. I got too excited and didn't act right. I'll be back in just a few minutes."

When Junebug sat down and started eating, Bluebird stared at him until he looked up and saw her staring. "I'm sorry, Granny, but you pretty much told my news."

"Well, you can answer some questions for me."

Junebug paused in the act of buttering his corn. "Like what?"

"Like how did you find out Henry is coming home?"

"Oh, I saw him and his family at their old home place on the way home. His mother and sisters was cryin when they saw what them bad men did to their place, but Henry's dad just said they could camp out until they got the house rebuilt."

"The women probably didn't like that. They are likely tired of camping since they have been doing that very thing on the Red River for the last three years."

June's eyes got big. "How did you know that, Granny?"

Jim snorted. "You're young, son. Believe me, women always know how other women think. Now, what exactly did Henry say?"

"He said he hoped he could get his job back because his family really needs the money."

Star shook her head and sighed. "I wish I could hire him back, but we just can't afford it. We're just barely scraping by as it is."

Andrew, who had been quietly listening, spoke up. "Ain't you forgettin something?"

"What am I forgetting?"

"You still have them pay envelopes you have been savin for me."

"That's true, but that's your money. I can't use it to pay wages."

"Why not if I tell you that's what I want it used for?"

"Are you sure? It doesn't seem right."

Andrew grinned so wide that he showed the hole where he once had a front tooth. "Miss Star, if it weren't for your pa and your husband, I would be layin drunk in some ditch somewhere, or maybe even dead. It would make me real happy that I can pay you back a little."

Jim leaned over and patted Andrew on the back. "I'm right proud of you, Andy."

Star smiled. "So am I. All right, I will use your money... but only on one condition."

"What's that?"

"We will get it out of the safe tonight, count it, and record how much is there. Then we'll keep track of every penny I pay out to Henry."

"That sounds fine to me, Miss Star."

"Just one more thing. Someday, when we're prosperous again, Sam will pay every penny back to you with interest."

"We'll just wait and see, ma'am."

"Yes, we will."

Henry rode over the next day and reported to work. After the noon meal, Bluebird was sweeping the back porch when she heard someone whispering in Cherokee. Listening attentively, she determined the sound was coming from behind the big forsythia bush that grew by the right side of the porch. When she peered into the bush, she startled two small girls who were hiding there. "Why are you children hiding in the bushes?"

The smaller of the girls, who looked to be seven or eight, began to cry. "Please don't tell Brother Henry we are here."

The older girl stood up, and Bluebird's eyes watered when she saw the thin arms and legs that protruded from a ragged outgrown dress. She grabbed the younger girl's hand and pulled her up. "We're sorry, ma'am. We'll leave right now."

The little girl jerked her hand away. "But I'm hungry, sister, and you said we could pick something to eat from their garden when no one was looking. "

The little girl threw herself down and wailed. Bluebird rushed to her side and put her arms around her. "Don't cry, little one. Both you girls are welcome to come inside and eat."

The older girl shook her head and turned to walk away. "No, we don't beg for food. Now listen to me, sister. It's time to go."

Bluebird raised up and faced the girl. "No, you listen to your granny, young one. You aren't begging if it is freely given. Come in the house and eat. After you finish, you can help with the housework. I could use a couple more pairs of hands around here. What are your names?"

"I'm Theda, and my little sister is Pearly. Could I ask you for a favor?"

Bluebird smiled. "That depends. What's the favor?"

"We need to leave before Henry comes for supper. If he sees us here, we'll be in trouble."

"I think we can arrange that."

Bluebird loaded Henry down with leftover food from supper. When he protested, Bluebird said, "I cooked too much today, and I don't want it to go to waste. Your family might as well help us eat it."

Henry smiled and thanked her. He never questioned Bluebird again but grinned and took the food each time it was offered. His little sisters came back three or four times a week until it was almost time for school to start. Each time they came, Bluebird noticed an improvement in their appearance. Neither girl was plump, but they had lost the emaciated look they once had.

As the days went by, and Sam didn't come home, Star began to worry. One morning when she and her mother were eating breakfast on the front porch, she asked, "Ma, where is he? The war ended almost two months ago. Do you think something happened to him?"

"No, I feel in my heart that he is on his way home, but something caused a delay. Maybe he has been sick or hurt."

"Lord, I hope not!" Star began to cry. Then she wiped her eyes. "As long as he gets here. That's all that matters."

AN EMACIATED SAMUEL Clay lay in a hospital bed in Leavenworth, Kansas, feverish and restless. "Hey, Doc. When are you goin to let me out of this place?"

"Soldier, ask me that again when you quit running a fever."

"But I'm feelin fine! Let me get on my horse and ride home!"

"I would be committing murder if I allowed you to get on a

horse. Your leg is still infected, and you will be lucky if we are able to save it. Now, I must take my leave. I have many more patients to attend to."

The man in the next bed complained, "Clay, if you don't shut your mouth about goin home, I am goin to shut it for you!"

"McClain, if you think you can, come on over here, and try it!"

A stern-looking nun interrupted the argument. "Both of you men, hush! Doctor Couch will dismiss whomever he chooses to dismiss when that patient is ready and not a minute before!"

Sam apologized. "I'm sorry, Sister. It's just that I haven't seen my wife in nearly three years, and I know she is worried sick about me. She probably knows the war is over and wonders why I'm not home yet."

"Perhaps you should write her a letter."

"Well, now that my mind is clearer, I might just try that. Do you have anything to write with?"

"I will see what I can do after I finish my rounds."

Doctor Couch finally deemed Sam well enough to be dismissed from the hospital three months after the war ended. As soon as he got the good news, he sold his father's gold watch to hire a coach to take him to where Rowdy was stabled. With what was left over from the watch sale, he paid the stable bill and bought provisions for the journey home.

THE FIRST TWO hundred miles or so were tiring and slow but passed without major incidents, other than heavy rains, which delayed him for an additional four days. Now, after almost four weeks of travel, and within thirty miles of home, Samuel Clay was fighting for his life. He had been careless that morning, and now he was paying the price. He heard there were bushwhackers who had been looting and killing all during the war, and he suspected they were likely still preying on any lone travelers that they came across. But when he shot a fat rabbit close to the road, his hunger got the best of him. First, though, he took care of his horse. Although his stomach was growling, he led Rowdy to drink from a nearby creek and gave him some grain that he carried in his saddle bag. Then he found a shady spot several yards from where he was planning to roast the rabbit and tied him securely to a tree. He hadn't lit a fire for the last hundred miles of his journey until now, and he was smiling in anticipation of a real meal. He quickly skinned the rabbit, attached its body to a stick he had cut, and roasted it. He could barely wait until it was done to cut off some chunks of meat. He had only eaten a couple of bites of the juicy rabbit, when two grizzled men, wearing tattered, filthy Confederate uniforms rode up.

Sam's heart pounded. They looked exactly like he had pictured bushwhackers in his mind—hard, cold men who wouldn't mind killing him. The older one smiled and showed his crooked, tobacco-stained teeth.

"Hello, friend. What you eatin there? Looks mighty good."

"Just a rabbit I shot this mornin. I'll be glad to share it with you."

"Why, don't mind if we do, mister. In fact, we need you to share that fine lookin horse you got tied up over yonder and course everythin else you got!"

The man had barely finished speaking when Sam got off a shot that struck him in the temple, killing the bushwhacker instantly. Then he dived behind a nearby tree as the man's companion fired on him.

After a few more shots were exchanged, the bushwhacker quit firing, and Sam took advantage of the lull to call out. "You know, feller, this fight ain't necessary. Nobody else needs to get killed. Why don't you just ride away, and we'll forget this ever happened."

"Sure, I'll ride away, and you'll shoot me in the back!"

"No, I won't, but if you don't trust me, I'll toss my gun over by the fire. But, in case you get any ideas about shootin at me, I will tell you, this throwin knife I have is pretty deadly."

"That sounds fair enough. Just stay where you are for a few minutes while I get gone."

Sam breathed a sigh of relief as he heard the bushwhacker's horse make its way through the trees. He stood up, retrieved his gun, and heard the bushwhacker cackle. "Thank you kindly for this nice horse and saddle. Hope you enjoy my old nag!"

Sam swore and got off two more shots, but the bushwhacker had already ridden off on Rowdy.

Why had he lit that fire this morning? If he hadn't, he might still have his favorite horse and still be on a fast track home.

Sam patted the neck of the scrawny mare. "Well, hello old girl. Looks like you've been treated pretty rough. I promise you that I will treat you nice if you will just get me home to my wife."

THE NEXT MORNING, Bluebird noticed that Star didn't eat her breakfast. Instead she took a cup of coffee and sat on the front porch swing, swinging slowly and looking down the lane that led to the main road.

"Star, you need to eat something. You don't want to be sick when Sam comes home."

"Just not hungry, Ma. I dreamed about Sam last night."

"If it was a good dream, tell me. If it wasn't, keep it to yourself. We don't want to speak aloud of bad things less they come true."

"It was good, Ma. In my dream, Sam was riding on an old nag that could barely carry him, but he was over close to Fort Gibson."

"Fort Gibson is about twenty or so miles from here, isn't it? If your dream is partly true, on Rowdy, he could be here sometime late tonight or early in the morning."

"All true, part true, or false, I'm going to sit here as long as I can see and wait for him."

"You know my mother, Lame Bird, also had prophetic dreams, but even if your dream is true, you will need to eat and get some rest."

"Please, Ma. Just let me sit in peace."

"All right then."

Bluebird fed Junebug and the hired hands two more times, and

Star ate a small portion each time. June asked, "What's wrong with Ma? All she does is sit on the porch."

"She's just got a lot on her mind."

"Is it all right if I go out in the woods and check for deer signs while there's a little light left?"

"Go ahead. Just get back before dark."

When the moon appeared in the sky, she heard Star shut the door and come into the house. "Guess it will be tomorrow. Good night, June. Good night, Ma. I'm going to get ready for bed."

"Good night, Ma. See you in the mornin."

The next morning Star took her coffee and her place on the porch swing. Jim asked, "Is she goin to sit there all day again today?"

"I think so. It doesn't do any good to ask her to come in."

"Well, I hope Sam comes pretty soon, or his wife is goin to worry herself sick over him."

Several hours later, Bluebird proved she still had good hearing. "Listen, is that a horse I hear?"

"Glory be! I believe it is! Look, ma'am, she's standin up and wavin her hand! It must be Sam ridin up. We better go meet him."

"No, Jim. Let Star greet him first. We can wait."

Junebug came running in from the woods where he had been hunting with Ox. "I knew Pa was home! Old Ox started barkin and carryin on. Why is everybody just standin around? Why ain't you runnin out to meet him? Well, I ain't waitin."

Jim put his hand up to stop him. "Your granny said to give them some time to themselves."

June shrugged his shoulders. "All right. But I don't see why."

"You will someday."

Star found that she couldn't wait for Sam to come to her. She picked up her skirts and ran down the dusty lane. "Sam! Sam! You're finally home."

As she ran toward him, she took in his appearance. "Sam, I have never seen you looking so skinny and so whiskered!"

Sam pulled back on the reins and brought his steed to a halt. He ran his hands over his thick red beard. "Well, this hairy face will be shaved clean before this day ends, and as for being skinny, that won't last long either, as soon as I get to eatin your ma's cookin. Honey, even though you are boney, you are still a sight for sore eyes! Here, hold the reins while I get off this old nag. Rowdy was stole from me by a sorry bushwhacker, and this old mare was all that was left for me to ride home. Come here, darlin, and let me kiss you! I've been seein you on this front porch for three years now. I used to look at the stars every night and think of you, waitin for me here."

Then he stumbled and almost fell. "What's wrong? Are you hurt?"

"That's nothing, just a little souvenir that the Rebs gave me at Newtonia. Then I got shot again almost in the same place in a skirmish near Leavenworth, and my leg got real infected. I can't ride a horse as long as I used to. That, plus losin Rowdy, slowed me down considerable. No need to fret. Most days my leg don't even pain me. Now quit your worryin and come here."

Star and Sam embraced, and he gave her a lusty kiss. "Oh, Lordy, how I have missed those sweet lips of yours!"

"And I have missed you, Sam! I have been looking at the stars every night, too, and longing for you. Please promise me that you will never leave me again."

"That's an easy promise to keep, Star. Hey, is that Junebug standing over there? He's almost grown up! Come here, son, and give your old pa a hug."

Tears streaming from his eyes, Junebug ran to hug his father. "It's good to see you, Pa."

"And it's good to see you, son. Would you do me a favor? Would you get this nag to the barn and give her something to eat and a good rub down? I made her a promise I intend to keep."

After June left, he turned back to Star. "Time to say howdy to everybody. I'm starvin to death but mostly for you."

Star knew in her heart the night Sam returned from the war was the same night their only biological child was conceived.

V

YOUNG SAM

ON THE MORNING of July 4, 1866, an overdue, greatly swollen Star had just waddled out onto the front porch when the pains hit her, hard. She fell to her knees with a gasp, and Sam looked at her with alarm and squatted beside her. "What's wrong, Star? Is it the baby?"

Star managed to get out a hissed affirmative, as the bag of waters spilled and pooled around her. "Oh, Lord! Let me get your ma. Bluebird, where are you? The baby's comin!"

Bluebird ran to his side. "It will be all right, Sam. The first one usually takes a long time. Go get some old rags to clean this up. But first, help me get her in bed and then you need to send Henry to ride over and get Kohene Fivekiller. She delivered Star, and she is going to deliver her baby."

Twelve hours later, Kohene told a worried Blue, "She has such narrow hips, and the baby has broad shoulders. I am afraid your daughter is going to have the same trouble you did having babies. Maybe more."

"I wasn't any bigger, but Star was a small baby."

"Yes, and this one takes after his father."

Star come out of her haze of pain long enough to say, "Remember I still understand Cherokee, and I know every word you are saying. "

"Oh, I am sorry, Star. I didn't mean to worry you, but I did forget for a minute. I have delivered a lot of babies, some of them a lot bigger than this one. It will be all right. It's just going to take a while."

Star hissed through clenched teeth. "How much longer?"

"There's no way to tell. Go ahead and scream if you need to. Sometimes it helps."

"I believe I will." Star let out a blood curdling war cry.

Sam, who was pacing on the front porch, began to sob, "My God, she's dyin!"

Junebug started crying. "I don't want Ma to die!"

Jim patted Sam on the shoulder and handed June a dirty handkerchief. "Listen, men. I know it sounds awful bad, but it will be all right. My wife's had four, and she screams like she's dyin ever time."

Bluebird maintained her calmness until Star got quiet and still. "Star, Star! Are you all right?"

Kohene shook her head. "She's tired out, and it's not time to push yet."

Bluebird sighed and said, "I am going to pray for a while, but I'll be back soon."

As she passed by his room, she saw June staring into space. "June, go to bed."

"All right, but promise to wake me up if somethin happens."

Bluebird walked to the small stream that ran beside the spring house. She knelt on her knees as she remembered Grandmother doing. Then she prayed, "Creator, don't get angry, but I am going to pray to the Christian God now. Christian God, please give Star the strength to have her baby, and let them both live. If you will answer my prayer, I will go to your house every Sunday, and I will do what the white preacher tells me to do. *Wa-do*, and thank you in English, too."

When she walked into the room where Star lay sleeping, she shook her roughly. "Wake up, Star! It's time to have this baby right now!"

Star opened her eyes, moaned, and closed them again. "Ma, go away and let me rest."

"You have rested long enough. This baby has got to get born. Take my hand, bear down, and squeeze hard every time you have a pain."

Three hours later, at 11:45 p.m., a large, brown, baby boy came into the world, crying lustily. His grandmother washed him in warm water and swaddled him in a tight, small, blue blanket. Then she looked into his dancing dark eyes. "Hello, Grandmother Wolf, I see you in there."

Then he smiled at her, like he had a happy secret.

She told the exhausted mother, "Star, you have a strong son, who has eyes like Grandmother Wolf. Here, you can hold him, and I will go get Sam before he breaks the door down."

She walked out to the porch. A pale, shaking Sam said, "I heard the baby crying. Is it over?"

"Yes, you have a big, smiling son."

"Thank God! How is Star?"

"She is fine. Just tired. You can go see them both."

Kohene talked quietly to Bluebird. "She shouldn't have any more babies. It was very hard to get the heavy bleeding to stop. I will mix up a tea for her to drink every day so she won't get pregnant again."

"Thanks, Kohene. I will tell her in a few days. Right now, let her just enjoy Dancing Eyes."

"Is that his Cherokee name?"

"Well, really it's 'Wolf with dancing eyes', but I will call him 'Dancing Eyes.' Guess I better go see what his white name is."

Bluebird walked into Sam and Star's bedroom and beamed at the happy scene. Sam was holding Star's hand and gazing at his son with tears in his eyes. "He's sure handsome, Star. I'm glad he looks more like you. Look at all of that black hair!"

Bluebird laughed. "Huh! He didn't get those big shoulders, hands, and feet from Star. I don't know how tall he will be, but he's not going to be small-boned like his mother."

Star counted the little fingers and toes. "All there. Well, I hope he looks a lot like Sam, and I want to name him after Sam and my pa. What do you think about Samuel Greyson Clay?"

"It's a good name. That way you honor both men."

"That's fine, Star, but won't havin two Sam's around be confusin?"

"We can call you Samuel and call the baby Sam."

"That should work. Hey, he was born on the Fourth of July, wasn't he? Let's shoot off some guns and light some fireworks to celebrate."

"Oh, that's why his eyes danced, and he smiled."

Samuel turned his eyes from the baby to stare at his mother-in-law. "What do you mean, Bluebird?"

"When I first looked into his eyes, they were dancing, and he smiled at me. Just like Grandmother Wolf when she had a happy secret. That's why his Cherokee name is Dancing Eyes."

Star stroked the soft baby cheek. "I like that, Mother. But what is his secret?"

"He chose to be born on the night of the Fourth of July so everyone will make a special celebration for him."

Samuel chuckled. "We sure have a lot to celebrate. Let me tell Jim and Andrew and wake up Junebug, and we'll get the celebration goin!"

Bluebird's young grandson was the joy of her life. She told him stories about his grandfather, his great-grandfather, and his great-grandmothers, all in Cherokee.

His father sometimes complained. "Star, all Sam wants to do is sit and listen to those old tales of your ma's. He needs to be out more, learnin how to do things."

"Leave him alone. We waited almost seven years for that boy, and if he wants to sit and listen to his granny's stories, he can just do that."

Samuel looked at his beautiful wife and relented. "All right. Have it your way, but don't blame me if he turns into a lazy no-account."

Bluebird took him to his first stomp dance when he was four years old. She had taken June the first three years he had lived with Star and Sam, but he had taken himself after that. Star fussed about her taking Sam, but Bluebird said, "Dancing Eyes needs to know about his people, and since you won't take him, it's my responsibility."

"You used to make me go with you and pa, and I liked it when I was little. The food is good, and the stickball game is fun to watch. But I always got tired before all the dancing was over, and I hated that drink you made me drink when I got older. It was so nasty!"

"That's to purge you of the bad things in your body and spirit."

"I just know I hated it. I haven't been to a stomp dance since before I married Samuel."

"Well, you know you are welcome to come with us."

"No, I have better things to do. Just make sure that little Sam doesn't come home with mosquito bites all over him."

Bluebird scoffed. "You and Junebug never had mosquito bites, and neither will he. I have a good mixture for that."

Junebug liked Sam well enough, but with fourteen years difference in the boys' ages, they had little in common. He occasionally played with baby Sam, but he got annoyed when Sam got old enough to want to follow him around. He would say, "Granny, could you make Sam quit doggin my steps? I can't do nothin with him underfoot."

Bluebird would scold and tell him, "As the elder brother, it is your responsibility to teach him about Cherokee ways."

"But he's too little to understand any of that. Warrior and me are goin on a ride."

When Sam was five, and June was nineteen, their father announced that he and June were taking some cattle to Kansas City. It was June's first cattle drive, and he could barely contain himself. He told Bluebird, "It's goin to be grand, bein out on the trail, with Warrior and Pa and the rest of the fellers."

Bluebird smirked. "Don't forget all of the smelly cows and the pesky mosquitos."

"Oh, Granny, I don't mind the smell, and I'll take some of your special mixture for the bugs."

Star kissed both of her men and admonished them to "be careful." She watched Junebug ride off beside his father on a new horse he had trained. "Warrior's going to miss June."

Little Sam spoke up, "June asked me to take care of him while he's away. I'm gonna give him an apple every mornin and brush him every night."

Star ruffled the boy's thick, shiny black hair. "That's good, Sam. That way Warrior will have another boy to love and care for him."

"When will they come home, Ma?"

"Oh, they'll be gone for some time, but we'll be so busy taking care of the farm that time will pass faster than you can imagine."

WHEN THEY STOPPED for their midday meal, Samuel climbed off of his horse and nearly fell. Andrew grabbed his arm to steady him. "Easy, Boss! You ain't used to bein in the saddle that long."

"That's for blame sure! Think I better spend the rest of the day ridin in the cook wagon. Tie my horse up, would you? Tell June to come over for a word."

In a few minutes, Junebug, looking fresh and slightly perplexed, approached his father, as he sat eating. "Pa, I was surprised when you called for a halt. I believe we could have done another hour or two easy before stoppin."

"Maybe you could have, son, but my bad leg was painin me somethin fierce, and my belly was growlin for food."

"Sorry, Pa. I get to ridin, and I just get carried away sometimes. There's just no better feelin in the world than ridin across the open country on a good horse."

"I can understand how you feel. That's just your nature, but don't forget that not everybody can keep up with you. We got a lot of miles in front of us, and we can't wear out our hands or our stock before we get to the end."

"I'll try to do better."

"I know you will. Say, I got a notion of somethin that might work for both of us. Sit down here and eat with me, and I will tell you about it."

Samuel remained silent until he had eaten his last bite of food and drank his last drop of coffee. He pushed aside his dirty dishes and explained his plan. "First of all, I am goin to quit tryin to prove that I can ride like I used to. Most days I'm goin to be ridin beside Lovett in the cook wagon. It's easier on this broke down old body. Since you like to ride fast, I'm goin to let you scout ahead with Martinez. He's the best rider and the most experienced man I got. You report back to me pronto if there's any danger ahead or anything else I need to know."

"Sounds good, Pa. Talk to you at supper."

Then, before Samuel could get himself over to the chuck wagon, he was gone, in a smooth, fast glide of a ride. Sam and Lovett, an old friend and decent cook, traded stories all afternoon. "That boy of yours is a natural, Sam. He takes to the trail like he was born to it. Don't be surprised if he don't go home with you."

"Well, I grant you he's mighty good with horses. Did you know he blanket trained a bronc in one day when he was only ten years old? Ever hear of such a thing?"

"Can't say that I have. He looks to be good with a rope, too. I noticed he ran down a wanderin steer, roped him, and brought him back to the herd in just a few minutes' time."

"Yep, he's a talented youngster all right, but I still think he will want to go home to see his old horse and eat his granny's cookin'."

Except for the usual mishaps, the drive was smooth until they crossed into Kansas. Samuel knew they were in trouble when June and Martinez came back, riding like the Devil and his imps were on their trail. June rode up to the chuckwagon, hollering in Cherokee. "Easy, son. Tell me in English."

"Pa, there's a bunch of men waitin to ambush us less than five miles ahead, and they started shootin as soon as they caught sight of us!"

Samuel signaled for the hands to keep the cattle in a stationary position. Then he asked Martinez, "Do we stand any chance at all against them?"

Martinez shook his head. "It's doubtful."

"Can we get around them?"

"Maybe if we had time."

Junebug couldn't keep still. His nervous pacing brought him to a standstill in front of his father. "Pa, let me buy us some time."

"How?"

"I can lead them away."

"Oh, no, boy. You'd wind up getting killed when they caught up with you, and then your ma would kill me. There's got to be another way. We got to talk our way out of this somehow."

"They ain't interested in talkin. That's why they tried to kill us."

"Or maybe they just didn't want to talk to the two of you. Did you get a look at them before you rode off?"

Martinez spoke up. "Looked to me like about fifteen to twenty white men."

"Come to think of it, they was all white. And what was really peculiar, they was all wearin old Confederate uniforms."

A small grin started growing under Sam's thick red mustache. "You don't say? I think I might just see a way out of this. Time to go talk to some bushwhackers."

"That could be dangerous. Let me go with you, Pa."

"Not this time. I don't want them to know you and Martinez have any part in this outfit."

Junebug looked like a small hurt boy. "I don't understand. Why?"

"It ain't got nothin to do with you men. It's them bushwhackers. They hate anyone with dark skin. That's why they shot at you. Besides, I got an important job for you two to do."

A few minutes later Sam and Lovett led the herd down the road. At exactly where they were expected to be, two grimy, tobacco chewing Confederates stopped them. "Hold on there, men! You got to stop and pay the toll."

Sam appeared to be surprised. "What toll? Who are you men?"

"We serve under Captain Janeaway, and the toll is our rightful due."

Sam chuckled. "Well, gentlemen. You do know the war is over, and your side lost?"

A third, more reputable looking man, had joined the duo. "I am Captain Janeaway, and my men continue the fight to end the northern aggression. Of course, they still have to eat, and that's why we collect the toll from all large parties who pass through here."

"Well, I only see three men. What's to stop us from killin you and goin on our way?"

The captain raised his rifle, and a company of twenty men took their places behind him. "I only see about ten cowhands with you men, so I think you are outgunned. Now, all we are asking is fifty cents a head, and you look to have about three thousand head."

"More like two thousand."

"All right. I'm a reasonable man. We'll compromise at twenty-five hundred. How much would their toll be, Bishop?"

"Looks like twelve hundred and fifty dollars."

Samuel sputtered. "I ain't got that much cash money on me!"

"I told you I was a reasonable man. We're all honest white gentlemen here, so an arrangement can be made. Give me five hundred dollars and five hundred head."

Samuel let out a string of curses. "We might all be white, but we sure ain't all honest! I can't afford to give you five hundred head."

The captain took off his hat and wiped his brow with a white handkerchief. Then he smirked. "You don't really have a choice, do you? Think of it this way. We could just kill you all and take what we want."

"Not without losin a bunch of your men first."

"True. I love my men, and they love me. That's why they have stayed with me all these years. All right, what do you propose?"

"Two hundred dollars and two hundred head."

In a flash, the captain pulled out his pistol and pointed it at Sam. Immediately Lovett and the hands nearest Samuel drew down. "Don't insult my intelligence, sir! Now make a reasonable offer."

Samuel took off his hat and slowly wiped his brow and face and held out his hands. "Men, put your guns away! All right. You can have your five hundred dollars, but I can only afford to give you three hundred head."

The captain put his gun down and extended his hand for a hand shake. "Done. Allow my men to take my cattle and give me my money, and you can be on your way."

Samuel gave a deep sigh and shook his hand. "All right. Live and learn I guess. I know not to come back this way."

"I wouldn't expect you to. Nice doing business with you."

As Samuel was counting out the money, one of the captain's men came riding up. "Them cattle are sure stringy. It weren't easy to find three hundred good head."

"Well, a bargain is a bargain. Goodbye, sir. I wish you good fortune on the rest of your drive."

"Thank you, I guess. If you don't mind, we're goin to water the cattle we got left at that branch up ahead before we leave."

"Help yourself. Just don't linger."

"Don't worry. We won't. I'm as anxious to leave as you are to have me leave." Samuel yelled out to his hands. "Head em up, boys!"

A few minutes later, out of the sight of the retreating bushwhackers, Samuel rejoined June and Martinez down at the stream. "Well, I'm glad we bought you enough time to get my best cattle away from them bushwhackers. Have any trouble handlin five hundred head by yourselves? "

Martinez grinned. "No, you put your best hands on the job, didn't you?"

Samuel slapped Martinez on the back and ruffled Junebug's hair. "Guess I did. Now hurry up and help me get the rest of them cows watered before the bushwhackers come back and catch us."

Ten miles from Coffeyville, they came into the vicinity of another cattle drive. Martinez and Junebug rode back and told them the news. "Boss, we need to slow these cows down. Charlie Goodnight has a herd that is twice as big as ours just a mile or two up the trail. He said he would like to meet up with you when you get to Coffeyville."

Junebug's fingers and toes were drumming a nervous tune. "Pa, can you fix it where I can meet him?"

"Sure can, son. I ain't seen Charlie in a long time, but I reckon he will remember me."

That night, after the cows had been put in the stockyards, Samuel and Junebug saw Goodnight sitting with two of his men and Martinez in the hotel dining room. He stood up and waved them over to his table. "Sam Clay, I heard you were on the trail again. It's been a long time. Come on over and eat a bite with us."

Samuel and Junebug sat down and Sam shook Goodnight's hand.

"You're right about that. We weren't much older than Junebug here when we rode together. This is my son, Junebug Clay."

Goodnight shook June's hand. "Your son? I didn't know you was old enough to have a boy this age."

"He saved my life and adopted me, Mister Goodnight."

"Well, that explains it. Say, Junebug, Martinez tells me you handled yourself pretty good on the drive."

Junebug shrugged his shoulders. "Did the best I could, but I sure did like it, sir."

"Did you, now? That's good. What would you think about joinin up with my outfit?"

Junebug beamed. "I would be right honored, sir!" Then he looked at his father. "That is if it would be all right with you, Pa."

Samuel laughed. "Guess Lovett was right. You ain't comin home with me."

STAR CRIED AND scolded Samuel for letting Junebug leave. Bluebird said, "All mothers have to lose their sons sometime. At least it helps to know Junebug is happy doing what he was meant to do."

"He just better come home for Christmas."

"Didn't Samuel make him promise that he would?"

Star blew her nose and dried her eyes. "He just better not forget."

Star cried again when Junebug told them goodbye after spending a week with them at Christmas. Junebug turned to young Sam. "You've done such a good job takin care of Warrior, I believe he thinks he's your horse now, so I'm givin him to you."

Young Sam grinned. "Thanks, June."

Sam shook his hand. "Good luck, son. Come back and see us when you can."

"Come here, boy. I got something to give you." She handed him a pair of leather moccasins. "I made you these so you can give your feet a rest from those heavy boots you wear all the time."

"Thanks, Granny. They're just what I needed." Then he gathered her in a big hug, mounted his horse, and rode away.

The first two years June was away he and Star exchanged monthly letters. He didn't make it home again until two more Christmases had passed, but he always sent a big box with presents for his parents, young Sam, and Grandma Bluebird.

Meanwhile young Sam Clay grew to be a strong, dark, handsome young man, quick to laugh, and always ready with a story to tell or a song to sing. His easy-going disposition began to change when he first saw Redbird Smith at a stomp dance. Sam noticed that, during one of the breaks, a large group of men were gathered in one of the arbors, talking in Cherokee. Then a sinewy man, with piercing black eyes and a thick bushy mustache, stood up to get their attention. Sam walked over so he could hear what the speaker was saying.

"Cherokees, the white man is talking about giving each of us an allotment of land. Don't take it. All of this land is ours, and we should live on it as a sovereign people. If you take their bribe, you are admitting they had the right to drive us from our homes and can still control our lives. They told us all of this land would be ours, and now they are going to parcel it out to us as they want? We are Cherokees, and we have the right to live as Cherokees, not as puppets to a white government!"

Smith went on to make several other points about the necessity of refusing the land allotment and keeping to the old ways. He urged them all to join his society of Keetoowahs. Sam listened to the entire speech, along with several other Cherokee men, who were nodding their heads in agreement as Smith spoke.

Sam noticed a tall striking Cherokee with shoulder-length hair, listening intently to Smith's every word. From time to time, he would nod his head and murmur his assent. Smith stopped talking and pointed his chin toward where the man sat. "We have a Cherokee Senator here tonight, Ned Christie."

Christie nodded and threw up his hand to greet the listeners. "I am always interested in listening to a fellow Cherokee speak, especially when he speaks the truth. My family came over the Trail, like many others who are here tonight. We learned the hard way not to trust the white man. Redbird is right. Cherokees should refuse the land they offer."

One young Cherokee, in the back of the crowd, said something in response, but Smith couldn't hear him. "Speak up, young man. My ears aren't as keen as they once were."

Christie turned his commanding dark eyes on the speaker and said, "Yes, I am also interested in hearing your thoughts."

Several other men, sitting near the young man, encouraged him to stand up and talk. He resisted at first, but finally, stood up and spoke in a quiet voice. "The whites treated us shamefully. Now it is time they make amends by giving each of us land. I will sign their papers so my family can have their share."

Smith smiled indulgently. "May I ask you a question, young man, before I respond to what you said?"

"Of course."

"How did your family get to Indian Territory?"

"They came on their own before Jackson forced them out."

"So, they were what some call 'Old Settlers'?"

An angry buzz went through the crowd, and Sam feared for the young man's safety. Smith held up his hand, and the buzz died away. "All Cherokees are welcome to speak here. Go ahead and say your piece."

The young man looked around as if to check the mood of the crowd before he finally spoke. "Yes, they were Old Settlers, and I am not ashamed of them. They just did what they thought was best at the time."

Ned Christie rose to his feet and deflected the attention of the crowd. "You are right to not be ashamed of your family, and what has happened in the past cannot be changed. But those who walked the Trail passed on this truth to their descendants. Never trust the white man. Now I must be on my way to my home in Wauhillau. Chief Bushyhead has called a special meeting in Tahlequah tomorrow, and I need to get ready to go. Before I leave, let me give you men some advice. Listen to Redbird Smith. His words are wise and true."

Sam danced that night like he always did, but his feet were leaden. His mind kept wandering back to what Smith and Christie had said. Were all white men liars? His own father was white, and he had never lied to him or to any man, as far as he knew. Samuel Clay had a good reputation in his community. Many had called him a war hero, and Sam would agree. He suspected some of his father's health problems were related to the wounds he had received in the war. But maybe his father was an exceptional white man. There were other white men in the community who called Indians drunken savages and said they didn't have enough sense to take care of their families and belongings. Sam suspected this kind of thinking was their justification for robbing the Cherokees of the land they had been promised for moving to Indian Territory. As daylight approached, he watched as the blood of the white rooster was poured on the coals of the sacred fire.

He once asked an elder the significance of the white rooster as an animal sacrifice. The old man looked at him out of the corner of his eye and grinned a toothless grin. Then he chuckled and said, in Cherokee, "Grandson, look closely at the color of the rooster and look what is done to him. Now, who do you think the white rooster signifies?"

Sam grimaced and wondered at his mental slowness. Of course, the rooster was the white man. Then he considered the hidden hate his people continued to hold against the whites. His granny spoke about what she and others had endured on the Trail, but he never detected hate in her voice, resentment, yes, but not hate. Maybe he didn't understand because of his granny's attitude and the love his white father and his Cherokee mother had always shown each other.

Although Bluebird said she was too old to go to stomp dances anymore, she still took a keen interest in what happened there. The next morning, at breakfast, Sam told his family what Smith and Christie had said. Samuel said, "Sounds like good speeches, but who would refuse free land? If it is ever offered to you, I want you to take it."

Star nodded her head in agreement. "Yes, son. Even though it is a pittance of what our people are owed by the white man, it is a payment of a sort for the pain they caused us."

Sam turned to Bluebird. "What do you think, Granny?"

"I am thinking of what your grandpa, Grey Wolf, would have said. He would have supported Redbird Smith and Ned Christie and refused the land. If he were here now, he would have become one of these Keetoowahs."

Samuel put down his cup of coffee and glared at Bluebird. "Yes, but who can turn down free land? This Keetoowah movement will die out soon, and I don't want Sam to get mixed-up in it."

Sam said, "Guess I have a lot to think about."

It wasn't long before Bluebird showed her family that age had done nothing to dull her quick thinking. His father insisted Sam accompany him on an overnight trip to Fort Gibson. His eyes misted over as he explained his old commander was going to be honored at the fort for his service to his country during the Civil War. "His health is failin, and he sent letters to all his men, askin them if they would come to the ceremony. It will probably be the last time we see the Captain alive, and I want my son to meet him."

"Pa, I'll be glad to go with you, but do you think it's safe to leave Ma and Granny here alone? Didn't I hear there's been reports of outlaws in the area?"

"They won't be alone. Jim, Henry, and Andy will be here, and I told them to keep special watch while we are gone. "

Right before they rode away, Samuel motioned for Star to come to him. "Star, you might keep my gun close by, just in case."

"I will."

He leaned from his horse and kissed her. "Be careful. "

"You do the same. See you soon. "

"Goodbye, Ma."

"Goodbye, Sam. Take care of your pa."

"I will. You and Granny take care of yourselves."

"Don't worry about us. Just have a good time."

After she fed the dogs that night, Star walked into the house, looking for her mother. Bluebird was sitting in her rocking chair in the parlor, her lower body covered with a quilt, reading her

Cherokee Bible. She looked up and smiled. "Star, did you know this Bible belonged to Grandmother Wolf? It's the only thing I have that belonged to her. Would you like to read it?"

"Maybe later. My mind is so tired I don't think I could make out the Cherokee words right now."

"All right then. Go to bed."

"Aren't you going to sleep?"

"In a little while. I want to read a bit more."

"All right. See you in the morning."

As Star left the room, she could hear her mother reciting in Cherokee. "For he shall give his angels charge over thee, to keep thee in all thy ways...."

She lay down and was almost asleep when she heard the backdoor creak open. Jim always knocked and announced his coming so she suspected an intruder. Reaching across, she uncovered the rifle from the quilt on Sam's side of the bed and cocked it. As she eased out of bed, she saw a man's hand, holding a gun, protrude around the corner of the bedroom door, and his other hand began to slowly open it. She fought to control her trembling fingers as she aimed the rifle.

Then a shot rang out, and she screamed. She cautiously opened the door.

The outlaw lay still, bleeding from a bullet hole in his right temple. Star gasped at the sight of her petite mother standing beside the corpse. "I got him before he could hurt you, Star. I would never let anyone hurt you."

Jim, Henry, and Andrew, who were on watch outside the house, came running in, guns in hand. Jim yelled, "What happened?"

"Oh, nothing much. Ma just killed an outlaw."

Jim chewed on his mustache a while before he finally spoke. "Well, I tell you what I want to do. I heard tell Bass Reeves is in Tahlequah, and I would like to go fetch him early in the mornin. They say Judge Parker sent him to our area to catch the outlaws that's been stealin and killin in this part of the country. This one might be one he's been lookin for. Is that all right with you, ma'am?"

"Yes, go ahead."

The next morning Star was in her bedroom getting ready for the day when she heard a rumbling bass voice in the kitchen. She hurriedly changed her clothes and brushed her hair. Her mother was serving biscuits and gravy to the hands and a tall black lawman, who stood when she entered the room. "Good mornin, Missus Clay. Heard you had some trouble with a bad man last night."

Jim stood up and pointed toward the lawman. "This here's Marshal Bass Reeves. I explained how your ma killed the outlaw to keep him from hurtin or killin you. He's goin to take a look at him and haul him back to Fort Smith. Oh, Marshal, I found this big knife on the body. Is it all right if I keep it? It's a mighty fine blade."

Reeves shook his head. "Sorry, Jim. I gotta turn it in to Judge Parker, along with the Colt, as evidence. Missus Clay, do you mind if I borrow a horse to tie the body on? I will leave it at the livery stable for you to pick up next time you go to town. I got a pack mule at the stable that I use for transportin prisoners and bodies, but he threw a shoe yesterday, so I couldn't bring him today."

"That will be fine. We appreciate your help, Marshal Reeves."

Then to Star's surprise Reeves went to where her mother was sitting and took her hands in his. He began speaking to her in Cherokee. Bluebird's eyes glowed, and she smiled as she conversed with him for several minutes."

"Well, how about that? I heard tell Reeves could speak Cherokee. What are they talkin about?"

"My Cherokee is rusty. Do you know, Henry?"

"I think he told Miss Bluebird she is a very brave woman and a good shot. He thanked her for helping him catch the bad man and for the good breakfast. She told him he was welcome to come by here anytime and eat with her, and he could tell her stories in Cherokee about all the bad men he was catching. She said it was good to have someone to talk Cherokee to again."

Reeves' rumbling laugh came deep from his belly, and Bluebird laughed with him. "That's a pretty good translation, son, but you left out the part where she said she would pack me some vittles to eat on the way. Thank you, ladies, for your help. You will be hearin more from me in the future. I will send word to Sheriff Sixkiller at the Cherokee Prison in Tahlequah when I learn the identity of this culprit. He will let you know who it is and if there's any reward money or not."

Bluebird said, "Just a minute, and I will have some food for you. Star, sit here and eat your breakfast and visit with the marshal while I get his vittles."

In a few minutes, she returned with a large bundle of biscuits. Speaking in Cherokee, she said, "Some of these have cold ham, and some have fresh apple butter. I hope you like them."

Reeves leaned down, kissed her cheek, and said, "Wa-do." He tipped his brown Stetson. "It was good to meet you, ladies, but I must get on to Fort Smith."

Smiling broadly, Bluebird turned from the window where she had stood to watch Reeves ride away. "Too bad he's married, but I couldn't stand that big mustache anyway."

When Sam and his father came home, Sam couldn't believe what Granny and Ma told him had happened. How could his little granny shoot a cold-blooded killer? When he asked her how she did it, she shrugged her shoulders and said, "Anybody could do it. His attention was on getting into your mother's bedroom so he didn't see me with my gun aimed at him.'

Samuel was almost as shocked as his son. "I didn't know you even had a gun. Where did you get it?"

"It was Grey Wolf's. Molly taught me how to shoot it when I was just a young girl. She was a crack shot and saved my life once. Someday I will tell you that story, Dancing Eyes."

Samuel gently hugged Bluebird. "However it happened don't matter. I am just thankful that you saved my Star."

Bluebird grinned and pushed him away. "She was my Star first."

Star laughed and hugged first her mother and then her husband. "I am just glad to be here right now."

A week later they had a visit from the Cherokee Sheriff, Sam Sixkiller. Bluebird saw him first, riding up the lane on a big bay gelding. "I think another lawman might be coming. This one's not as tall or as good-looking as Bass Reeves, but he has the look of a lawman about him. "

Samuel went to the door to greet their visitor. "Hello, Sheriff. Good to see you again. How can I help you?"

"Bass Reeves sent word for me to give your mother-in-law a hundred dollars for your assistance in the capture of Edmund Driscoll. He was wanted for helping rob three banks in Missouri and for the murder of a teller. He had a two-hundred-dollar bounty on his head, and Bass said he figured she earned half of it. He said he would pay me back next time he came this way."

Samuel motioned for Bluebird to come to the door. "Here's the woman who shot the outlaw. She earned that reward money."

Sixkiller chuckled and shook Bluebird's hand. In Cherokee, he said, "Wa-do, Grandmother." Then he put a big envelope full of money in her hand.

Bluebird giggled and said, "Good! Someone else I can talk Cherokee to. Come in the kitchen, Sheriff, and have some breakfast."

Bluebird continued to be a major influence in young Sam's life. They spent hours discussing the old days and the dilemmas facing Cherokees in modern times. She doted on him, never finding fault with anything he did. His father and mother often fussed at their youngest son. Sam wasn't ambitious enough, would rather sing than work, and didn't show any interest in courting girls, all great failings in their minds.

One evening she called him to her room and handed him an object wrapped in brown paper. "Go ahead and open it. It's yours now."

He opened it and stared at its contents. "A rock. Why are you giving me a rock?"

"It's not just any rock. That is the stone I took from the stream, near the cave where I hid in Georgia. I carried it all the way from Georgia to Indian Territory on the Trail. I always meant to give it to your mother, but she never seemed interested in hearing the old stories and the old ways. When you came along, I knew I had saved it for you. Today is the day I am supposed to hand it down to you. Someday that day will come to you, and you will pass it on to one of your children or grandchildren."

"Thank you, Granny. I am honored, and will always take care of it."

"I know you will, Dancing Eyes. Oh, here's another gift I have been keeping for you." She handed Sam a heavy, hand-carved wooden box.

"That's a little too pretty for me, Granny."

She clucked her tongue at him. "Junebug sent it to me for Christmas last year, all the way from Texas."

"Then you should keep it. It's your gift."

"Just open it."

He opened the box to reveal one hundred dollars in notes and silver. "Granny, this is the reward money you earned. You shouldn't give it away."

"I want you to keep it until a day you really need it. Now good night."

"All right. If you change your mind, just tell me. Good night."

As he prepared a bedtime snack that night, his mother came to the kitchen, where he was sitting, to have a word. "Sam, I swear you never pay attention to anything! Didn't you notice how the song leader's daughter was smiling at you in church this morning?"

"Was she, Ma? I think Minnie Proctor likes to smile at everybody. She's just like that."

Bluebird came downstairs to speak in Sam's defense. "Leave him alone. The Creator will show him the way when it is time, and he will find the right girl at the right time."

"Ma, if Sam listens to you, he will never get married! Oh, well, I'm tired. Let's all get some rest."

The next morning Star called upstairs to him, "Sam, get up. Wake-up your granny so she can eat breakfast with us."

When he went to wake up Bluebird, he noticed she was lying very still. As was his custom, he spoke to her in Cherokee. "Granny, get up. Breakfast is ready." But she didn't rise up in the bed and grin at him as was her morning habit. He touched her hand, and it was cold. She was gone.

He sat by her bedside for just a minute, looking down at her beloved face. "Granny, I will never forget you. Thank you for teaching me what it means to be a Cherokee. I am going to find Redbird Smith and talk to him myself. I think you would like that."

Then he brushed the tears from his eyes and went downstairs. Star looked up as he came into the kitchen. "Where's your grandma?"

He walked to where she was sitting and put his hands on her shoulders. "Granny's gone."

Star gasped, stared at him in disbelief, and shook her head. "No, she's not! She's just in a deep sleep. I'll go wake her up."

Samuel put out his hand to help her up. "Come on, Star. I'll go with you."

Sam watched his parents walk up the stairs. A few minutes later he walked outside to escape his mother's wails. He met Jim running to the back door. "Is somethin wrong with your ma?"

"It's all right, Jim. Ma's cryin because Granny just passed away."

After giving Sam an awkward hug, tears welled-up, and Jim used the back of his hands to wipe them away. "I'm sure sorry, boy. Your granny was real special, and we're all gonna miss her."

Sam watched as the undertaker and his assistant came to take his grandmother's body to the funeral parlor. "Ma, aren't we goin to have a wake for Granny like we did for Grandpa?"

"No, your granny was a member of the Presbyterian Church just like we are. She gave up those old ways a long time ago. She would want a regular Christian service."

"But she took me to stomp dances when I was young."

"That was just so you could learn about your culture, and I really didn't approve of that."

"How about all her friends who went to the stomp dances with her? Aren't you goin to tell them about the funeral?"

"I really don't know their names or how to reach them."

"I know some of them. Do you mind if I tell them?"

"No, I don't mind as long as they know we aren't going to have a wake or follow any of the old customs. You can tell them the funeral will be the day after tomorrow, Friday, at ten o'clock at the Presbyterian Church."

"How about June?"

"Your father sent a telegram to the sheriff of Amarillo to tell him about his grandma, but who knows when he will get it and when he can come home?"

Sam rode over to Katie Springwater's house to tell her. Katie's daughter-in-law met him at the door. "She's sleepin now, but I will tell her as soon as she wakes up. I'm sure she will have me take some food over to your place to give our respects. Kate doesn't get out much anymore."

Her eyes softened, and she patted his hand. "I'm sorry you lost your granny, Sam. She was a fine woman."

"Yes, she was. Do you know of any elders that still practice the old ways?"

"There's not many of them left. You might go to the Keetoowah. I can tell you where Redbird Smith lives."

"Please do."

When Sam arrived at Redbird's house near Vian, he was waiting at the gate. "Si-yo, young Sam. Did you come to ask me more questions?"

"No, sir. This time I am asking for your prayers."

"For yourself?"

"No, for my grandmother. She passed away this morning."

"I know your grandmother. Her name is Bluebird. I used to see her at all the stomp dances."

"Yes, she used to go when she was able."

"Do you want me to arrange a wake for her?"

Sam hesitated. "No, my mother doesn't want a wake. Could you just say the ceremonial prayers for her here?"

Redbird patted him on the shoulder. "I understand. I will pray for Bluebird."

"*Wa-do.* I appreciate it. Would you mind lettin the other Cherokees who attend stomp dances know about the funeral. It will be at ten o'clock on Friday morning at the Presbyterian Church."

"I will see that they know. Come back next time with questions for me."

"I will."

Almost all of Bluebird's friends had passed away so most of the funeral guests were contemporaries of Sam and Starr. Bluebird lay in repose in her fine mahogany coffin, surrounded by fresh flowers, at the front of the church. Just as the preacher took the pulpit, the back door opened, and several older Cherokee men and women filed in. They sat on the back two pews of the church. Star whispered to Sam, "Who are they?"

"Granny's stomp dance friends."

Star grimaced as she shook her head. "I should have known."

The funeral was quiet with the only sounds being the preacher's voice and Star's soft crying. At its conclusion, the last two rows of people filed by the coffin. Sam's heavy heart lightened when he heard Granny's friends speak to her in Cherokee.

VI

SAM AND MARY

DESPITE HIS PARENTS' protests, Sam continued to listen to Redbird Smith and consider joining the Keetoowahs. His parents' determination to run his life was a source of frustration for Sam, but he tried to be patient with them. One morning, he came home after daybreak and found his father, sitting by the fireplace, waiting for him. "Gettin in mighty late, Sam. It's almost time for the hired hands to be stirrin around doin the mornin chores."

"This is about the usual time I get in from a stomp dance. You just usually aren't up, waitin on me."

"Well, that's true enough. But I been wantin to talk to you sometime when your mother's not around."

His father's statement puzzled Sam. "Is something the matter?"

Samuel hesitated for a minute. Then he took a deep breath and began speaking. "I reckon you could say that. So, here it is, plain and simple. The fact is I'm gettin older, and my body has started actin up. It's got to the point where I can barely walk to the barn anymore without gettin winded. I don't talk about it to your mother because I don't want to worry her, but I know what I know. My father died before he was sixty, and I think I am goin the same way."

Worry and fear swept through Sam, but he forced a calm demeanor. "Then you need to go to the doctor, Pa, and see what can be done."

"That's not what I want to talk to you about, son. How old are you now?"

"I am twenty-one. What has that got to do with anything?"

Samuel blushed and cleared his throat. After an uncomfortable silence he said, "You know that the happiest day of my life was the day you was born. I don't want to die without seein you have that same experience."

Sam shook his head in disbelief. "So, that's what this is all about? Just another jab at me for bein single! I seem to remember Granny told me you were near to thirty before you married Ma."

Sam chuckled and shook his head. "I was twenty-five. Remember your granny always said white people look older than their years? But you got it all wrong. I just had somethin I been wantin to tell you, so I did. Never mind then. Go on to bed."

Sam saw his father's sad face as he started to walk away. Then he recalled what Granny had said when he complained to her about his parents, "Dancing Eyes, you must always remember who you are to your parents."

"Who am I?"

"Have you ever seen a hen that has only one chick?"

"Yes, a time or two."

"A hen with just one chick spends all of her time clucking at her chick. She doesn't let him out of her sight, which probably worries the chick almost as much as the hen."

He was his father's only chick, his most precious possession.

"Hey, Pa!"

His father turned around. "What?"

"Don't give up on me. I'll find the right girl someday, and you'll get to be a grandpa yet."

The sadness lifted from his father's face, and he grinned. "I sure hope so, son."

A few days later, Sam speculated as he washed up for Sunday dinner. *Wonder who Ma has brought home from church for me to meet today?*

As he walked into the kitchen, he caught a glimpse of a stunning young woman sitting across the table from his mother. His usual indifference melted away when he sat down beside her. At least this one is pretty and Cherokee.

His mother was beaming. "Here's our Sam now! Sam, I want you to meet Mary Elk. She is from Saline, or some people call it Salina, but she is visiting her kinfolk in Tahlequah this summer and helping out in church on the weekends."

"*Si-yo*, Mary."

Mary returned his greeting and added several more remarks in Cherokee. Sam smiled in delight and continued the conversation for several minutes.

Sam finally noticed the pleased look his parents exchanged but ignored them. He was having a good time talking to the pretty girl. Ma waved her hand to interrupt them. "All right, Sam. Please start speaking in English, so that your father and I can join in."

"Oh, sorry, Ma. I just don't get the chance to talk Cherokee in this house much, and I took advantage of the opportunity."

"I am sorry, too, Missus Clay. I will try to remember to speak in English, so everyone can understand."

"Mary, you can call us Samuel and Star. No need for formalities. Thanks for understanding about the communication problem. I spoke Cherokee when I was young, but over the years, I have forgotten most of it. Of course, being white, Samuel never learned it. You can speak all the Cherokee you want when it's just the two of you talking, which I am sure you will be doing a lot. I promised your mother to bring you home with us from church for Sunday dinner every Sunday this summer. Sam, you don't mind hitching up the buggy to take us back for Sunday evening service, do you?"

"No, I don't mind at all."

DESPITE HIS PARENTS' misgivings about his knowledge of the opposite sex, Sam was experienced in romancing young women. He once met a girl named Ahniwake at a stomp dance and nearly brought her home to meet his parents. She was a full blood and very pretty, and they liked to talk, laugh, and kiss. The night he was going to ask her, she wasn't there, and he looked everywhere for her. When he finally asked one of her sisters about Ahniwake, he was told that Ahniwake had to stay at home until she learned to only fall in love with another Keetoowah. This incident kept Sam away from stomp dances for a few months, but when he went back, he saw Ahniwake sitting in her clan's brush arbor. She only gave him a cool nod when he spoke to her. He made a resolution to stop trying to find romance at the stomp dances or anywhere else.

But with the arrival of Mary, it wasn't long before Sam was accompanying his parents to church every Sunday morning and most Sunday evenings. He loved to listen to Mary play the piano during the song service, often joining in lustily when the congregation sang. One Sunday Pastor Scott asked, "Mary, why don't you and Sam sing a special for us next Sunday?"

"We can do that, can't we, Sam?"

"I guess we can."

AT DINNER, Sam teased. "What did you get us into, Mary?"

"What's wrong, are you backing out on me?"

Samuel slapped him on the back. "He most certainly is not! My boy knows better than to break a promise to a lady."

Star agreed. "That's right, and as soon as we finish dinner, you two can go to the parlor and practice. Pa can help me clear the table and wash the dishes today."

Sam liked sitting close to Mary on the piano bench. She smelled like fresh-cut flowers. When he bent to turn the page of her music, he couldn't resist giving her a peck on the cheek. "What was that for?"

"That was a little kiss for a pretty lady. Did you like it?"

"I didn't mind it."

"Well, let's try a bigger one."

Sam and Mary didn't finish the song for several minutes, and he realized he had found the woman he wanted to share his life with. His parents both grinned when they finally came back to the kitchen. Sam and Mary continued to court the rest of the summer, and by its end, Mary took Sam home to meet her family.

Although no one said anything negative, Mary's family, especially the men, didn't seem as happy as Sam's parents were. Her parents accepted Mary's decision, but her father didn't have much to say to Sam. Her brother, Alex, who asked to be called by his Cherokee name, Tall Elk, let Sam know they were all Nighthawks.

Sam was puzzled. "I have heard of Redbird Smith and the Keetoowahs, but who are the Night Hawks?"

Tall Elk scowled. "Nighthawks were once Keetoowahs who saw the need to break away from Smith and follow our own way. I always thought my little sister would marry one of her own kind."

"If it's important to Mary, I will consider joining."

Oddly enough, it was Mary who finally turned him away from becoming a Nighthawk. One day she said, "Sam, I don't want to marry a Nighthawk. I have seen what a hard life it is for my mother, my sisters, and my brother's wife. I want to marry a Cherokee man who is just as hard-working and prosperous as any white man. They owe us more than they can ever give us, so let's take land, money, or whatever they offer."

Sam put aside his feelings and quit listening to Redbird Smith. Whenever he saw Smith at stomp dances or elsewhere, Smith would just frown at him and shake his head.

Mary was a welcome addition to the local stomp dances. Her mother had taught Mary how to make plump, golden fried pies, filled with delicious cooked juicy fruit or savory meat. She brought a batch to the first stomp dance they attended as a couple, and they were gone within minutes. The other young men gave Sam envious looks, and the older men all congratulated him on finding a woman who was a good cook. The older women welcomed another cook into their group and were soon telling Mary all they knew about cooking and managing a household.

Some of the younger women were not so welcoming. Minnie Proctor, in particular, gave Mary mean looks and whispered snide remarks whenever she saw her. Mary tried to ignore her by looking away, but then Minnie forced her to act. Mary had just emerged from relieving herself in the woods some distance away from the stomp grounds when she found herself surrounded by Minnie and three of her friends. Minnie, who was at least four inches shorter than Mary and about ten to fifteen pounds heavier, emerged from the circle to stand directly in front of Mary. Black eyes snapping, she sneered as she berated Mary in Cherokee. "You are not welcome at our stomp grounds, and you are not welcome to our men. Leave here and don't come back, or else you will wish you had!"

Then she pushed Mary, and Mary pushed back. Soon the two women were grappling on the ground while Minnie's friends called out encouragement. At first the heavier Minnie had the upper hand, and she held Mary on the ground while she slapped and clawed at her face. Then Mary managed to free one of her legs and kicked Minnie hard enough in the stomach so that Minnie gasped and rolled off her. The agile Mary, blood streaming from the wounds of her enemy, sprang to her feet and started kicking the prone Minnie. She kept on kicking her until Minnie's screams alerted the other attendees that something bad was happening in the woods.

When Sam saw what was going on, he rushed forward to stop it, but some of the older men held him back. "No, Sam, this is women's business. Let them take care of it."

One of the older women put her hand on Mary's shoulder and said, "You can quit now, Mary. You have won the fight."

Mary shuddered and fell into the woman's arms, sobbing. "It's all right, Mary. You did what you had to do. Come with me, and I will get you cleaned up."

Minnie's friends helped her up, and she ran off into the woods, crying. Her mother shook her head and went after her. Two of her aunts followed.

Sam stood around until the woman, who had helped Mary, came after him. "Mary is sitting in your wagon, waiting on you. You need to take her home now."

"All right."

As he turned to walk away, the woman put her hand on his shoulder, "Sam, we want you and Mary to come back again. You will both always be welcome here. Minnie and her kin agreed to not attend the next stomp dance to give things time to cool off, but you should come back and bring Mary. She was not at fault for what happened here tonight."

"I will see what Mary says."

Mary sat in the wagon, with her face covered by her shawl. When he tried to hug her, she pushed him away. "What's wrong, Mary?"

"You know what's wrong. I have shamed you, and you hate me."

"Is that what you think?"

"What else could I think?"

"Well, you're wrong. I am proud of you, and I love you with all my soul."

Mary raised her head and stared at him. "How can you be proud? We rolled on the ground, scrapping like two crazy cats. I will go back to Saline where I belong."

He put his finger under her chin. "You are like the old Cherokee women who fought beside their men, and I am proud to marry you."

Mary's luminous eyes filled with tears. "Really?"

Sam bent and kissed first her eyelids, her mouth, and her neck. "Oh, yes."

They went back to the next month's stomp dance. Everyone welcomed them, but the older men all teased Sam about "finding him a wildcat." One elder said, "Wildcats are beautiful, but you need to stay on the good side of their claws."

When it was time for the dancing, he sat in the Bird Clan arbor, waiting for Mary. He heard her coming before he saw her. The turtle shells tied to her legs made the familiar rattling sound. "Sam, what are you doing sitting here? Aren't you going to dance?"

"Not yet. I will a little later."

"Well, suit yourself. The shakers have been called, and I must go."

He watched her walk away and smiled. Someday he would tell her why he always waited to dance. It was because he got intense pleasure from watching her dance. She was so beautiful, dressed in the black wrap-around skirt, the white cotton blouse, and the red fringed shawl her mother had made her. When the dancing began, her body and the shells she wore moved gracefully and in perfect rhythm to the drum beat. He felt drunk with love and desire for her and the realization he would soon know her intimately, body and soul.

They missed the next stomp dance, the one Minnie Proctor and her family would be attending. Mary had chosen that month, September, for their wedding month. The wedding was held in the local community church, and the pastor of the church performed the ceremony. Mary's family insisted that, after the church service was over, a traditional Cherokee wedding should take place. As soon as the preacher said, "I now pronounce you man and wife," he stepped aside and allowed Mary's family to come forward.

First an elder from Saline blessed the couple and all the wedding guests. Mary's oldest brother came to stand beside her and handed her an ear of corn. Then, Star, with an uncomfortable look on her face, pulled a cooked venison haunch from a burlap bag at her feet, which she gave to Sam. Sam and Mary solemnly exchanged the food items. Finally, a blue blanket was placed on the bride and groom, individually. Then the blankets were removed, and a large white blanket was placed to envelop them as a couple. Finally, they drank together from the two-sided wedding vase, and the elder prayed a final blessing prayer.

Mary had explained the symbolism to Sam before the wedding. "You give me venison because the man is the hunter and the provider of meat. I give you corn because I am responsible for taking care of the garden and crops, which I make into food for my family. My brother will be our children's uncle, and his duty is to teach them the ways of our clan, which is why he will stand beside me. Of course, drinking from the common vessel shows our unity." Mary stopped talking and blushed.

Sam's eyes started their dancing. "Why are you blushin, Mary? Aren't you goin to explain the blanket part of the ceremony to me?"

Mary looked away. "You know what the blankets symbolize."

He put his finger under her chin so she had to look in his eyes. "Remember, Mary, I am ignorant about Cherokee traditions. It's your duty to teach me."

She swatted his hand away. "Oh, you aggravating man! All right. I will say it. We started out sleeping under our own blankets, but soon we will share a blanket and a bed."

He laughed and kissed her. "Now, what was so hard about telling me that? That'll be my favorite part of the weddin."

AFTER THE TWO families shared a wedding meal, Sam and Mary drove away in their wagon, filled with wedding gifts, to the house where Grey and Bluebird once started their married life. Sam carried his young bride across the threshold and into the bedroom and lay her on the new bed he had purchased several weeks before. Then he slowly undressed the magnificent, strong woman who had captured his heart and soul. He took his time teaching her the pleasures of love making. By the time Sam took her virginity, she was so intoxicated with love that she scarcely felt the pain that occurred.

Their first son William was born eleven months after they were married. The boy had the look of Mary's people, long and slim, with ebony hair, large dark eyes, and creamy beige skin. Nevertheless, his proud paternal grandfather proclaimed, "Looks just like Sam did, a chip off the old block."

Six months after William's birth, Samuel asked Sam to come with him, along with ten temporary hired hands, on a cattle drive to a ranch near Fort Smith. "When you was little, I took Junebug on a big cattle drive to Coffeyville. That's when he discovered he wanted to make a livin at it, and that's when he met up with Charles Goodnight. Last I heard he's Goodnight's ramrod and happy to be with him. This here's small taters in comparison, but I hear tell they pay top dollar for cattle. Too bad I ain't as young as I once was, and I will probably spend most of my time ridin in the chuck wagon. I could really use a good trail boss like you. "

When they crossed over into Arkansas, they met an Osage hunting party and found their way barred. One of the twelve men spoke English, and he came forward to parley with them. The huge Osage's black eyes flashed and he spat when he saw Sam. "Bah! Cherokee!"

Samuel held up his hand for peace. "This is my son, Samuel Grayson Clay. Yes, he is Cherokee, but he is also white. I know Osages hate Cherokees because you think they took your territory, but think about this, man. The whites took land from all of you."

The big man sneered. "You are giving me more reasons to kill all of you."

"Hold on now. Let me finish. Since us Whites took your land, we need to pay you back some. Now I don't want your land. I just want to cross over where you're huntin. If you allow me to do this, I will pay you good."

"How good?"

"Say, five head."

"Ten head and five rifles."

"Sorry, can't do that. You might be tempted to use them rifles on us."

The Osage spat again and looked at Sam. "Ten head and five rifles, and we don't kill the worthless Cherokee."

Sam could tell his father's anger was getting stirred-up, and he put his hand on his arm and whispered, "Don't get mad. He's lookin for an excuse to kill us all. Offer him twelve head, two rifles, and some ammunition in exchange for safe passage for all."

Samuel shook his head and whispered back. "I don't want to give them no guns."

"Pa, we got two rifles with crooked sights. They can't hit the side of a barn with either one of them."

Samuel nodded and turned a smiling face to the Osage. "This is what I am goin to do. I will give you twelve head, two rifles, and I will throw in some ammunition. Having a rifle is no good without bullets."

The Osage looked at the leader of the party and received a nod. "All right, but get that worthless Cherokee out of our sight."

"Done." Sam climbed into the back of a wagon, the bargain was struck, and they were on their way.

After they delivered their cattle to the ranch for sale, Sam and his father paid the men part of their pay so they had money to spend on lodging and food in nearby Fort Smith. Samuel looked at them sternly and gave them some words of advice before dismissing them. "Don't spend all your money on whiskey and women. You won't get the rest of your pay until we start home. There's a livery stable on Main Street where you'll want to keep your horses. Meet you there tomorrow at noon. Then we'll head back home. Any man, who don't show up, misses out on the rest of his pay, and he gets left."

After they ate a big breakfast at the hotel, Samuel offered to show Sam around the town. When they got near the courthouse, they noticed a big crowd. "Come on, son. People's as thick as flies at the courthouse. Let's go see what's goin on."

Everyone was clustered around the courthouse steps. Sam held on to his father to steady him as they pushed their way through the crowd. Sam recoiled in horror when he saw what the crowd was gaping at. "My God, Pa!"

"What is it, Sam?"

"They got Ned Christie's body tied to a board, and they're takin pictures of him like they're at a circus."

Samuel glanced at the gruesome sight and shook his head. "Did you hear Ned killed a U.S. marshal a few years ago?"

"Yes, I heard that, but I also heard it wasn't true. And that is what I believe. I heard Ned speak one time, and he seemed like an honorable man. I know Redbird Smith and other Cherokee elders spoke highly of him."

"Well, I didn't know Ned, but I knew his father Watt. He shod my horses for me once or twice, and he done a good job. I never heard nothin bad about him or his boy."

"Why did the whites put his body on display like that?"

"Well, you know Ned's been hidin out in the fort he built for about four years now. Guess them lawmen was so mad when they couldn't capture him that they got plumb proud of theirselves when they finally did. Course they had to blind him in one eye first and use a cannon and dynamite to get him, but they don't dwell on that part of the tale."

Sam took his father's arm and helped him move out of the crowd. "You know sometimes I just don't understand white men."

"Neither do I, son. I don't understand people period, of any color, but I do understand one thing about this old white man. I am mighty tired, and I am lookin forward to sleepin in my own bed in a few days."

"And I am missin Will and Mary. "

At the mention of Will's name, Sam brightened up. "Speakin of my grandson, I believe he might be disappointed if I don't bring him a present from the big city."

"Pa, he's only six months old. I don't think he expects you to bring him anything."

"You don't know that. He's extra smart. Already crawlin and talkin."

Sam grinned. "All right. Have it your way. It did seem like he was tryin to say mama the other day."

"See there. Next thing you know he will be sayin poppa. There's an old general store on Main Street that has a big variety of merchandise. We might pick up somethin for our womenfolk there too."

As they made their way toward Main Street, Sam noticed his dad was stopping every few minutes to rub his legs and rest. "What's wrong, Pa? You seem to be havin trouble walkin."

Samuel stopped and pointed to his head. "See all that gray hair up there? I'm turnin into an old man, and being in the saddle or even ridin in a wagon for three days didn't help. Guess we should have stopped by the livery stable and got the wagon to drive. Oh, well, too late now. Maybe I better look for a cane for me. Least we're almost there."

When they got to the store, Samuel stopped again to look in the large window. "Looky there! That's what Will needs. His own hobby horse to ride until he gets big enough to ride a real one."

"Pa, he ain't even walkin yet."

"Don't matter. He will be in no time."

As soon as they stepped into the store, Samuel called out. "Somebody get me that hobby horse out of the window. My grandson needs it."

A small bald clerk ran to procure the horse, placed it at Samuel's feet, and said, "Here you are, sir."

His next stop was at the material counter. "Hmmm…I like bright colors, don't you? Give me twenty-four yards of that red calico with the yellow flowers on it. Now I don't want it all together. Give it to me in six portions of four yards each."

Sam stared at his father, with his mouth wide open. "Pa, why in thunderation are you buyin so much material? Even if you're thinkin to buy it for Ma and Mary, they won't ever use that much material."

"It will come in handy. Just wait and see."

The clerks scurried around, smiling and eager to wait on the big spender. "Now, what's next? Give me about two dozen tobacco plugs, one of them fancy hand mirrors, one pound of lemon drops, one pound of peppermint sticks, and one stout walkin cane. Now wrap it all up for me, except for the walkin cane. I need that now. "

Sam just stared at his pa and shook his head. Maybe he should surprise Mary with gifts. He found a fancy pair of hair combs for Mary and a tiny wool hat for Will.

After their purchases were totaled up and paid for, his father handed Sam the large burlap bag that contained his purchases. "Here, carry this for me. Now, let's get a bite to eat, and by the time we're finished, it will be time to meet the men."

Two hours later, all ten men were there, but a couple of them looked hungover. Samuel ignored their condition and told them to get ready to head out. When they were nearing the place where they met the Osages, Samuel gave the signal to stop. He said, "All right, Sam. Give me the bag from the wagon, and you crawl into the back."

"All right, but can I ask what you're goin to do?"

"Just wait and see. You should be able to hear every word from the back of the wagon."

A few minutes later they were confronted by the same party of Osages. The big angry one was sent to talk to Samuel again. He scowled and said, "Those guns you gave us are no good! I don't see the Cherokee. Where is he?"

"I'm sorry about the guns. Oh, the Cherokee stayed back in Fort Smith. I thought we might see you fellers again, so I bought you some really wonderful presents." Samuel made a big show of opening the big burlap bag.

The scowl was replaced with a look of curiosity, and the rest of the Osages joined the interpreter. "Our head man wants to know what you have in the bag."

"I have presents for my Osage friends who will allow us free passage. Do you want to see what I bring to my friends?"

"Our leader wants to see the presents."

"First, I have the finest chewin tobacco for my friends, enough for all of them to have two plugs each." Samuel handed the package holding the tobacco to the spokesman, who gave it to the leader. The Osage leader took out a plug, put it in his mouth, and murmured appreciatively. Then he gave the remainder to another man, who put it in an empty saddle bag.

"Next we have something for your women folk to sew with. Beautiful material to make shirts, skirts, and whatever else you want them to make."

The material was exclaimed over and placed in another saddle bag.

"Now this is somethin really special. A fine lookin glass for your leader to get a good look at his handsome self."

The leader snorted, but he held it to his face and examined himself before giving it to his assistant.

Samuel stopped and looked at the interpreter as if waiting.

"Our leader wants to know if that is all."

"Is that not enough?"

"No, we want more to make up for the bad guns."

"Well, I might have one more special item, but I was savin it to take home to my family."

The interpreter crossed his massive arms and scowled. "He wants it."

"You folks drive a hard bargain. All right, but since it is so rare, I want the leader's promise of safe passage."

The leader smirked. "You have my word. Give it to me."

"Oh, Mister Leader, you can speak English? That's a surprise. All right. Last, but not least, somethin delicious—sweet candy. Care to try a piece, sir?"

The leader took the plug of tobacco out of his mouth and replaced it with a lemon drop. Then he tried a peppermint stick. He smacked his lips appreciatively and signaled to the interpreter.

"You may leave now."

"Please tell him it's been a pleasure dealing with him."

After they were well out of sight, Samuel stopped the men again. Sam climbed out of the wagon and mounted his horse, which was being led with the pack horses by one of the young wranglers.

"What did you think of my play actin?"

"I got to admit I'm impressed. Well, better do my job and check out the lay of the land."

About a year later, Mary gave birth to another son. When his grandfather saw him, he laughed. "This boy looks even more like you than Will did. Same head, eyes, and build. What are you goin to name him?"

"This time I agree with you. He does look like me and you. When the sun hits his hair just right, it has a glint of red in it. He had to get that from you, so we thought we would name him after you. His name is John Samuel Clay."

Samuel stroked the little palm and grinned when the baby grabbed his thumb. "He's strong just like you was. And you're right. His hair's got a little red in it. That's the Scottish blood comin out."

The Fort Smith cattle drive was the last big trip Samuel Clay made. More and more he turned the ranch and farm duties over to his son. Sam noticed his father now found a lot of excuses for riding over to visit his grandsons. Will and John could do no wrong, and their grandfather loved to spoil them. For Will's fourth birthday, Poppa presented him with a pony and a miniature saddle, specially made for his size. Will showed no fear. He ran into the corral and scrambled up on the saddle with just a minimum of assistance from Andrew, who was watching. He grabbed the saddle horn and yelled, "Go, horse!"

Samuel, who came up beside him, said, "Take it slow, cow hand. First Poppa needs to lead your pony to give him time to get used to you bein on him."

Will bounced in the saddle and laughed. Mary was standing outside the corral, holding John. "That must be a very docile pony to put up with Will's behavior."

"Yes, Pa said he sent the pony to Zeke Mason's house when he first got him. He said if the pony could put up with all of Zeke's kids handlin it and tryin to ride it, then it would be gentle enough for Will."

Mary gave a worried sigh. "Your pa only made it one round before he handed the pony over to Andrew to lead. He looks all tired out."

"I think he feels a lot worse than he lets on. Maybe I can help Ma talk him into goin back to see Doc Adair."

"Good luck. He said he wasn't goin back because Doc Adair couldn't heal old age."

A few weeks later Samuel was confined to his bed. He sent word for Sam to come and bring his family. Sam tried to cheer his father up. "What's this I hear about you stayin in bed all the time? Have you got lazy in your old age?"

Samuel grinned, but when he spoke, his voice was weak. "Not my idea, son. Doctor's orders. Can't breathe. I do have an idea of my own, though, and I want to run it by you. Pour me a glass of water first, would you?"

Samuel's hands shook as he took the glass from Sam's outstretched hand. He slowly drained the glass and gave it back to his son. Then he took a deep breath and resumed speaking. "I want you to move your family into my house. You could use the room, and your mother could use your help in takin care of me. And as for me, I could use more time to watch my grandsons play outside my window." He took another deep breath and looked at Sam and Mary to see their reaction.

"We'll need to talk about it first."

Mary put her hand on top of Sam's hands. "No, we don't. If this is what your father wants, we should do it."

Samuel looked at her through misty eyes. "Thank you, Mary."

Samuel Clay spent his last days, sitting in a chair by his bedroom window—on good days. He laughed at the antics of his grandsons as they ran and played. Sometimes, when he felt like talking, he would talk to his son about things that needed to be done at the ranch. On bad days he would sleep and dream of happier times.

One chilly November morning, Mary came to his room with a stack of hot buttered flapjacks. "Thought you might like something sweet for breakfast this morning." She arranged his breakfast tray across his lap and hesitated before she poured topping on the flapjacks.

"I brought sorghum and honey. Which do you want?"

"Honey. Got any coffee?"

"Of course, and cream and sugar. I brought me some coffee, too, so I can sit beside you. We can drink and talk together."

"I don't know if I can eat all this. Do you want some?"

"No, I already ate breakfast with the boys and Sam. He's out checking on some cows."

"How about Star? Did she eat with you?"

"Oh, you know Mother Star. She has a habit of eating breakfast out on the front porch."

He chuckled. "I plumb forgot! She got that habit watchin for me to come home from the war."

"So she told me. I have some news for you today, and you are the first to know."

Sam raised his bushy red eyebrows. "And what would that be?"

"I'm goin to have another baby."

He reached out and grabbed her hand. "That's good news. When will my new grandchild be born?"

"As near as I can figure, late May."

"Oh, a spring young'un. Spring's the best time of the year, you know."

"I think so too, but Sam likes the summer best."

"That's just cause his birthday comes then. I still remember that Fourth of July he was born." He sighed. "Thanks for tellin me, sweetheart. I just wish I could live until spring so I could see the new one."

She leaned over and wiped the corners of his mouth. "Maybe you can."

"Maybe so."

Samuel Clay died three weeks later. He was fifty-eight. Star threw herself into planning a nice funeral to honor her beloved Samuel. She bought the best coffin and ordered the finest tombstone. The church was packed the day of the service. Kinfolks, comrades in arms, friends, and acquaintances from all over showed up. Star hired extra help to assist Mary and her with the cooking and the serving of a huge funeral meal.

During the funeral, the preacher spoke at length about what an outstanding man Samuel was. When he asked if anyone else wanted to speak, several men stood to say a few words, including some of the men who had served with Samuel in the Civil War.

"I got something to say." A tall, well-dressed stranger, in a gray Stetson and shiny leather boots, walked to the front of the church, and every head in the place turned to see who he was. Mary asked Sam, "Who is that man?"

"I don't know, but he kinda looks familiar."

When the stranger got to the front, he swept his hat off with a flourish, and Sam recognized him. "It's Junebug, my brother."

"I just rode in from the Palo Duro Canyon where I herd cows for Mister Charles Goodnight. For them who don't know me, I am Junebug Clay, the son of that good man laying there in that coffin. This is the first time I have been home in a long time, and I am sorry for that because I didn't get to tell my father goodbye. I just hope somehow he knew how much he meant to me. If it hadn't been for Samuel Clay, divin into a fast-moving stream almost thirty years ago to save the life of a poor, skinny Cherokee boy he didn't know, I wouldn't be here. All I am or ever will be, I owe to Samuel Clay, and from the looks of this room, there are some others who owe him a lot too. Yes, Samuel Clay was a great man, and there ain't many like him."

Then he turned to where Sam was sitting with his family. "Mother Star and Brother Sam, I am sorry I didn't come home before this sad time. I missed Granny's funeral, too, didn't I? Writing letters just ain't the same, is it? Thanks, Brother, for sending me a telegraph message last week, tellin me Pa was getting bad. I was out on the trail, or I would have been here sooner. Now I have said my piece, and I will sit down and listen to the rest of the service."

Star stood up and said, "Come and sit with us, June."

Junebug smiled and walked from the front to where his family was sitting. Sam moved over to make room between him and his mother. Junebug shook his hand and hugged his mother.

Star smiled and hummed quietly when Mary and Sam tearfully sang one of Samuel's favorite hymns, "Amazing Grace." After he had wiped the tears from his eyes, Sam watched his mother and took note of her calm demeanor. He noticed, except for a few tears she shed when Samuel's coffin was lowered into the ground, his mother hadn't cried. It was hard for him to understand since even June, as tough as he was, kept dabbing at his eyes with his fancy white handkerchief.

When he helped her into the buggy to go home, he asked, "How are you doin, Ma?'

"Fine, Sam. I'm doing fine. Now hurry and get Mary and me to the house so we can help serve food and greet our guests."

Then she turned to Junebug and said, "I'm so glad you came, son."

"I wish I had got the news sooner, Ma."

"Well, it couldn't be helped so don't blame yourself."

Sam took Junebug aside when they got to the house and asked him, "Why ain't Ma cryin? Is somethin wrong with her?"

"She's just puttin up a good front for now. Are your children in the house? I been wantin to meet them, and I brought presents."

Mary chuckled. "Oh, they will be glad to meet you."

June's eyes shone with appreciation when he looked at Mary. "I never realized how smart my brother was until I saw you sittin by him. Ma wrote Sam married a pretty woman, but she didn't do you justice."

Mary blushed, and Sam laughed and squeezed her hand. Then in Cherokee, he said, "Careful, brother, you might make me jealous. You don't have to speak English to her because she speaks Cherokee better than I do."

June replied in Cherokee. "You found a treasure, brother. Now introduce me to my nephews." June was right about Star. After all the guests had left, and everyone was in bed, he heard his mother, crying and moaning. He knocked at her bedroom door and said, "Do you want to talk, Ma? Can I help?"

He heard her clear her throat before she answered him. "No, son. I need to be alone for now."

Everyone, except Sam and Mary cried when Junebug left a few days later. His mother kept hanging on to him, saying, "Why do you have to leave so soon?"

Even Will and John cried, and John said, "Why won't you stay and play with us some more?"

Junebug's face fell, and he said, "If you boys keep that up, you're goin to make me cry."

Mary patted the boys and said, "You will see your uncle again someday, and, Will, now you're old enough to write to him, and you will get letters back, all the way from Texas."

"And I'll do my best to answer them letters as soon as I get them. Just remember sometimes it takes quite a spell for them to get to me. Of course, I'll keep sendin Christmas presents like I do every year.

Hey, here's another idea. Why don't y'all come down to Texas and see me someday?"

John jumped up and down. "Hurrah! Let's go tomorrow."

Sam put his hand on John's head and said, "Simmer down, cow hand. We got to wait until your new sister or brother is born and gets big enough to travel."

After all the hugs and kisses were given, and all the promises were made, they all waved at June until he rode out of sight. When she thought no one was listening, Star whispered to Sam, "I know I won't see him again."

"Ma, that's foolish talk. Sure you'll see June again."

"I wish that were true, but it isn't."

On a bright May morning, Amelia was born. Star doted on the bright-eyed, raven-haired beauty. When Star held Amelia for the first time, she surprised Sam by bursting into tears.

"What's wrong, Ma?"

"Oh, nothing. I was just wishing your father could have seen this pretty little girl. He thought the world of your boys."

"Mother Star, he can see her. Probably the ones you called Bluebird and Grey Wolf can see her, too."

Star smiled through her tears. "I hope you are right, Mary."

Star was a big help to Mary before and after the new baby's birth. It wasn't long before she approached her son with a proposition. "Sam, your family has outgrown your little house. Why don't you all just plan on staying here, permanently. You could use the room, and I could sure use the company."

EVEN THOUGH HE missed his father, Sam considered himself to be one of the happiest and most prosperous men in their community. The only minor contention in his peaceful life was a difference of opinion about child rearing. Mary's family was much more traditional than the family Sam was brought up in. She insisted that Cherokee be the primary language spoken at their house and made sure that they thought of themselves first as members of the Deer clan. The summer after Amelia was born, when William was seven, Mary's solemn older brother, Tall Elk, came to their house. Sam greeted him heartily, as he did everyone. "Si-yo, it's good to see you. Come in and visit for a spell."

"I don't have much time, Sam. I came to take Will home with me for the summer."

"No one said anything to me about a long visit. "

Star, sitting in the corner of the room, knitting, heard the conversation. Speaking in her usual English, she said, "Will is too young to be away from his family for the whole summer. Why, he's only seven."

Mary and Will came into the room. In Will's right hand was a small bag. The wiry, dark-haired boy seemed nervous. He was biting his lip and trying not to cry. Mary called out cheerfully, "Will's ready to go, Uncle Tall Elk."

Star spoke up in indignation. "Surely, you're not letting him go, are you, Sam?"

"Mother and Tall Elk, would you mind letting Mary and me discuss this matter? Will, go play outside for a little while. Mary, let's go talk about this."

Will's countenance changed from darkness to light. He threw the bag down and ran out the back door, as if he were afraid someone was going to stop him.

Star muttered angrily under her breath and left the room in a huff. Tall Elk remained stony-faced and stared off into space. Meanwhile in the solitude of their bedroom, Sam and Mary were having a heated argument. "You never said a word about him goin anywhere this summer, Mary!"

"Yes, I did, and you shook your head in agreement!"

"Well, I didn't hear what you was sayin, or I would never agree to such a thing! Seven is too young to be away from home for a whole summer! Didn't you see how nervous the boy was?"

"In my clan, seven is a good age for a boy to start learning how to be a man from his uncle."

"I thought that was my job."

Mary rolled her eyes. "Oh, Sam, sometimes I don't even think you are a Cherokee! If you were, you would know that the mother's brother is responsible for training a young boy to be a good clan member and a strong man."

"Well, it's true I wasn't really raised in a clan, but I am a Cherokee and the head of this house. I have no problem with Will receiving instruction from his uncle, but as his father, I will say when he is ready to begin his lessons. Now, this is what we are going to do. Go tell your brother I will bring Will to his house in two weeks. Will can stay for a two-week visit. We'll see how things go. If things go well, we'll try a longer visit in the future, say a month. "

Sam saw the pout forming on Mary's full bottom lip and knew she was about to protest. He took her by the shoulders and looked deeply into her angry ebony eyes. "Now, pretty lady, I know you don't agree with me, but, as your husband, I ask you to accept what I decide. If we compromise, we can both get what we think is best for our family."

Things were cool between Star and Mary for a few days, but they eventually began talking easily again. Will came to enjoy his visits with Uncle Tall Elk and their clan family. By the time he was nine, Will was growing into a tall, lean young boy, who already had a reputation as a swift runner and a tough fighter. All of the men in his clan expected him to be good at stick ball when he was old enough to play. Will was also proficient with a blow gun and was always bringing home small game that he killed.

All in all, Sam and his family were happy, and their problems were small until the dark times came. It started one day when Will came home from school, feeling feverish. By the time he was diagnosed with the measles, John and Star had become infected, as did many others in their community. Will and John recovered, but Star did not, passing away quietly in just a few days.

Unlike her husband Samuel Clay's big funeral four years earlier,

Star Clay's funeral was a much smaller affair. All of the men in the community and surrounding area had known Samuel Clay, who had owned one of the largest farms around, and had fought with them, side by side, during the Civil War. The church had been packed the day of Samuel's funeral, and Star and Mary had cooked until the tables of Samuel's house were loaded down with food to serve all of the attendees.

Today, at his mother Star's funeral, the church was barely half-full. The measles epidemic had swept through the countryside, striking down young and old. The majority of those who remained were convalescing at home, like William and John. No one would be coming to their house for a funeral meal because Mary, who was expecting their fourth child, was busy taking care of her sick sons, as well as her healthy little daughter, Amelia.

After the short service, most of the people went home to check on their own sick. Only a few accompanied the pallbearers and Sam to the nearby graveyard. As Sam watched his mother's coffin being lowered into the ground, he felt a hand on his shoulder. He turned around to see who it was, and through his tears, didn't recognize who had touched him until he heard a familiar drawl.

"Sammy, I rode my horse all the way from the outskirts of Fort Gibson, just to come to Miss Star's funeral, and that ain't easy for a one-arm man."

"Jim Briggs, how are you? How long has it been, ten years? "

"Ever bit of it and more. You was still a bachelor when I moved my family to Fort Gibson. Say, I'm sure sorry I didn't come to your pa's funeral, but my wife, Pearl, was real sick at the time, and I had to sit with her. She almost died, but she's all right now. So, here you are, all grown-up with young'uns of your own. My kids are all grown-up too, and guess what?"

"What?"

"I got over twenty grandkids!"

"How about that? "Sam hesitated for a minute, wondering if Mary would mind, but then plunged ahead.

"Why don't you follow me home and eat a bite before you start back home. It may not be much since Mary's been busy with our sick kids, but you're welcome to eat with us. "

"All right, if it's not putting you out too much. I would like to see the old place again."

Sam thought Mary looked a little dismayed, but she smiled her pretty smile and hurried around to fry up some ham, eggs, and gravy to serve with some of the biscuits she always kept warm on the stove. Amelia had never gotten sick, and Will, being the first sick, was almost completely recovered. They both sat and ate at the table with Sam, Jim, and Mary. Will was old enough to take part in the conversation, but Amelia stared at the strange white man through her thick dark eyelashes and would just smile when asked a question. Otherwise, she was silent.

"Your little girl don't talk much, does she?"

"Sorry, Jim. Me and Mary mostly talk Cherokee in the house, and that's about all Amelia knows. The boys know English because they both go to school."

"Well, she's a pretty little thing, even if she don't talk to me. What's her name?"

Sam reached over and patted one of his daughter's soft cheeks. "This is Amelia."

"Well, that's a pretty name for a pretty little girl. Thanks, Miss Mary, for the vittles. They really hit the spot. I left the house early this morning and didn't have time for nothin but coffee."

"You're very welcome, Jim. Next time you come I will try to serve you a better meal with more food."

Jim stifled a belch. "Excuse me, ma'am. Why, I'm as stuffed as a hog now! I don't think I need more, and what I ate was real tasty. Say, Sam, remember how that Junebug could eat? Don't know as I ever seen anybody eat like that boy. He could eat four bowls of stew to my two. What ever happened to young June?"

"Well, you remember he always had a way with horses?"

"Don't I know it? I still remember that story Sam told about June ridin a horse that had never even had a saddle on it. I never heard of another livin soul doin that but June."

"Did he tell you about the bargain Granny made with Kate Christie to buy that horse for June?"

"I remember when it happened. That made quite a tale! But what happened to June?'

"Sorry, I got carried away telling stories. June went on a cattle drive to Coffeyville with Pa, and he really liked it. Then he met Charles Goodnight, and he wound up signing on with his outfit. He eventually became his ramrod and then his trail boss. Last I heard he had saved enough money to buy him a big cattle ranch somewhere near Abilene."

Jim laughed and slapped his knee. "Well, I'll be! Our Junebug turned into one of those cowboy fellers, and now he's a rich rancher."

"Yes, and he seems pretty happy. Ever six months or so we get a long letter from him, and he tells us all about his adventures on the cattle trail. He's met some famous people like Big Foot Wallace and Quanah Parker. I wish I knew exactly where he lives so I could get word to him about Ma."

"Can you believe it? Life sure is strange, ain't it? Hope you can find out where June is livin. Say, do you mind if I walk around outside a while? Brings back a lot of memories."

Mary extended her hand to Jim, and he grasped it. "It's been a pleasure meeting you, Mister Briggs. Of course, we don't mind. I would enjoy walking with you if I felt more like walking."

Jim's blue eyes twinkled as he looked at Mary. "When's your little one due?"

"In about three months, I think."

"Did you know I was there the night your husband was born?"

"Yes, Sam has told me. He told me so many stories about you that I almost feel like I already know you."

"And I'm right glad to know you. Well, you need to put your feet up and save the dishes for Sam. He can do them after he walks around with me for a while."

"Careful now what you volunteer me for."

Mary laughed. "You and Sam take all the time you need. Will can help with the dishes and cleaning up."

Sam walked around the property, listening to Jim's reminiscences. "Right over there's where you pa met your ma after he rode back from the war. You should have seen him, boney as a starvin wolf and just as hairy as one! And your ma was almost as boney. She about pined herself away, waitin on him to get back from the war. She had gone through some rough times, too. Did your ma ever tell you about the two run-ins with outlaws we had when Sam was away at war? They come close to killin us all."

"No, but Granny Bluebird did."

"That don't surprise me none. You know if it hadn't been for your granny, I wouldn't be alive today. She was one of a kind, that woman."

Sam felt himself choking up. "Yes, she was. I think about her every day."

"I know you do. Well, on with my story. Your granny Bluebird told us hands not to go botherin the two of them until they said hello proper, but they was still huggin when I got there. I never seen anybody love each other like those two did. Then about a year later they had you, and they was even happier." Jim took out his handkerchief, wiped his eyes, and blew his nose.

Sam's eyes filled up. He had to swallow before he could speak. "She tried to tell me once how much my parents loved me, but I didn't understand. Now since I have my own kids, I know what she meant."

"Well, Sam, that's just the way of life. You don't get all the answers at once. Some things can only be learned through experience, kinda like ridin a horse, which is what I need to be doin soon if I want to get home before pitch dark."

Jim grabbed Sam with his one good arm and hugged him. "Goodbye, Sammy. It sure was good to see you and this old place again. Maybe someday, if Pearl feels up to it, we'll come back this way. Take care of that pretty wife and them good-lookin kids. I didn't see the sick one, but he's likely good-lookin, too."

"That's John. Poor boy! He favors me except he has a flash of red in his hair. Got it from Pa. Sometimes his brother teases him about that. Built like a tack and a little clumsy, but he loves to sing and dance."

"Well, maybe I can meet John someday. You know, I know the soldier who runs the post office at Fort Gibson. He might be able to track June down for you. I'll send you word if I find out anything. Guess I better get on home. If you ever get over Fort Gibson way, ask where Jim Briggs lives, and some local will tell you. If I had time, I would draw you a map, but I better head to home."

"Thank you for coming, Jim. You don't know how much you helped me."

"I'm sorry you lost your ma, but I'm glad I could help, Sammy. So long now."

"So long."

Sam watched Jim's horse until it got out of sight, and then he went back into the house. He looked closely at Mary and saw the dark circles under her eyes. It looked like her feet and hands were swollen again too. He untied her apron and said, "Go to bed. The mites and I can manage without you tonight."

"Are you sure? John's still running a little fever."

"I know what to do. Go to bed."

A WEEK LATER, Sam went by the Tahlequah General Store for supplies. The clerk handed him a letter postmarked from Fort Gibson. "This came in yesterday with other mail and a delivery of goods from Fort Gibson."

Sam read the letter before he finished picking up his supplies. Jim had come up with June's new address and sent it to him. "Ma'am, do you have any stationery materials for sale? I need some writing paper, a pen, ink, and an envelope."

"Of course. That'll be twenty cents and a nickel for the postmark when you're finished. There's a bench outside if you need a place to write."

"Thank you. I'll have it back to you in just a minute to mail."

Sam wrote a short note, telling Junebug about the sudden sickness that had killed many, including their mother. He ended by saying, "I am sorry I couldn't send you word when she first got sick, but I didn't know where to write. Please come home and see us all if you can. Sincerely, Your brother Sam."

Two weeks later an apologetic Junebug showed up. By his side was a pretty young Mexican woman, holding a baby boy, who was the mirror image of his father. "I am so sorry that I haven't been home to visit and haven't even written a letter in over a year. Gettin married and havin a child is no excuse, but this is my wife Maria and our son Miguel."

Sam grabbed his brother in a fierce hug. "You don't have to apologize. What matters is you are here now."

Then he extended his hand to Maria and said, "Pleased to meet you, Maria. I had just about given up on my brother ever gettin married."

Maria and Miguel immediately bonded with their new family so much so that Maria refused to leave Mary's side when June prepared to go home. "I feel like Mary needs my help, and if it's all right with you, Sam, I would like to stay."

"Of course, Maria, you are welcome to stay as long as you want to. You're right, Mary is havin a hard time with this baby and could use your help and company."

June said, "Well, I will kinda miss them, but if Mary needs Maria, she can stay until after the baby is born."

The next morning Mary was so weak that she couldn't get out of bed. Sam sent for the man who was said to be the best doctor in Indian Territory, Dr. Lemasters. The doctor's eyes were solemn as he listened to Mary's heart and lungs and checked her swollen hands and feet. "May I speak to you privately, Mister Clay?"

Sam's heart beat fast as he waited for the dreaded words. "Your wife has worn herself out caring for her family. Her heart is very weak, and I am afraid pregnancy has added a tremendous strain to it. That's why she is so swollen. She must be on complete bed rest until it is time for the baby to be born."

"I will see that she stays in bed."

Sam sold two cows and hired a nurse to help Maria take care of Mary and the children. He spent most of his time sitting by Mary's bed side. Despite everyone's best efforts, misfortune struck in the last month of Mary's pregnancy. The baby, a little boy, came early, but didn't live long, despite being delivered by the respected doctor. They named him Alex after Mary's brother and buried him in the little family plot at the old homeplace beside Sam's parents and his grandparents.

Sam held a thin weak Mary in his arms and looked into her troubled dark eyes. "Sam, send Maria in to help me fix up. I want to see the children, and I don't want to scare them."

Sam felt relieved. Mary must be feeling better if she wanted to see the children. "As if you could ever scare anyone. I'll send Maria right in. Do you want Nurse Bidding, too?"

"Maybe later. Just Maria for now."

Maria was laughing and playing with the children while the nurse straightened up the house. When Maria saw his solemn face, she quit laughing.

"She wants you, Maria."

"All right. Let me get the nurse to stay with the children."

Sam opened the bedroom door and said, "Here's Maria."

"Come in, Maria. Close the door and give us a few minutes, Sam"

Twenty minutes later Sam knocked on the door. "Mary, are you ready to see the children?"

He heard Maria's cheerful voice call out, "We're ready, Sam."

Sam put on his happy face and went to the parlor where the nurse was reading a story to the boys, and little Amelia was playing with a doll while Miguel slept in a large basket nearby. "Ready to see Mama, kids?" Little Amelia hid her face in the nurse's skirts. Both of the boys said, "Yes."

The nurse put a marker in the book to hold her place. "We'll finish the story later, boys." Then she disentangled Amelia from her skirts and handed her up to her father. "Let me know when you need me, Mister Clay."

"Thanks, Margaret. I will."

Maria opened the door, and the boys ran in. Sam cautioned them. "Easy, boys."

Mary smiled, and her eyes looked bright and happy. "That's all right. Come and sit by me, boys, and tell me what you have been doing."

Will said, "I am learning my times tables. Ask me one."

"All right. What is five times five.

"Oh, that is easy, twenty-five. Ask me a hard one."

"All right. How about twelve times twelve?"

"One hundred and forty-four."

"That's correct. Good for you, Will."

John scooted close to his mother. "Ma, I have a new puppy."

"You do? What is his name?"

"Brownie because he's brown."

"Well, that's a good name for him, I guess. Are you taking good care of Brownie?"

"Yes, I feed him every morning and night."

"Come here, John. Give me a hug. You, too, Will."

Mary hugged and kissed the boys. "I love you, my darling boys. Now let me see your little sister."

"Come here, Amelia."

Amelia stayed close to Sam. He brought her over to the bed and tried to get her to take her face out of his coat. "Look at your mother, Amelia." Amelia immediately hid her face between her hands.

Mary put her hands over Amelia's. "Are you playing peek-a-boo, Amelia? All right. I'll play. Peek-a-boo! I see you."

Amelia giggled and removed her hands from her eyes. "Peek-a-boo, Mama!"

"Come here, sweet girl, and let Mama kiss you."

Mary kissed the little girl on her hands, face, and neck. For a minute, Mary's voice broke. "Oh, you smell so sweet, my baby!" She hugged the child close to her, shut her eyes, and inhaled the child's scent once again.

Then she smiled again. "Come here, boys. One more hug and kiss for all of you. Come here, Papa. I have a hug and kiss for you, too. Mama needs to rest now, but Papa, please come back and see me later,"

"All right. I will. Say goodbye to your mama, children."

The children said goodbye, and Sam told the nurse to go back in. Maria said, "I am going to check on Miguel." Then she leaned in close, and Sam could see the tears pooling in her eyes. "I am so sorry, Sam."

Sam tried to escape her sympathy. "Thank you, Maria, but it will be all right. Go ahead and stay with Miguel. I will take care of the children tonight."

Sam had just put the children to bed and was reading in the parlor when the nurse came and got him. "Missus Clay wants to see you now."

A few minutes later, he discovered the brave face was gone, and he held a weeping Mary in his arms. "Who will take care of our children, Sam?"

"You will, Mary."

Mary sighed deeply and closed her eyes for a few minutes. When she finally spoke, her voice was faint and hoarse. "No, my spirit is already drifting away. Promise me you will take care of them. The boys will be all right, but I worry about Amelia. She is so young, and she will have no woman to guide her."

"I will do my best to take care of Amelia and the boys, but, my darling, you are going to get well."

"No, Sam. We have never had lies between us, and I want no lies now. No, I am not getting well, and you know it. Give me your promise and kiss me one last time."

"I promise." Sam bent down and kissed her gently. He could barely hear her whisper.

"Wa-do, Sam. I am so glad we found each other."

Then she closed her eyes and passed away.

Sam clasped her close to his chest and sobbed, "No, don't go, Mary! I love you!"

VII

AMELIA

AMELIA NEVER FORGOT her first day of boarding school. When they first drove up to the formidable gates—the Gates of Hell she would later call them—she trembled. "Pa, what is this place?"

"This is your new school and new home."

"Did I do something bad, and you brought me here to punish me? I promise I won't be bad anymore. Take me back home, please!"

Sam took her hand and smiled at her. "Amelia, you will be better off here. I promised your mother I would take care of you, and this is the best way I can do it. It's been three years since she passed, and you need to be somewhere where you can get a good education, and where they can teach you to be a lady. You'll like it here after you stay awhile."

Amelia jerked her hand away. "I want to live at home and go to school with my brothers! Please, Pa!" Amelia began sobbing.

"Hush now, girl! You boys stay here with the buggy. Come on, Amelia, we need to go inside."

He helped her from the buggy and handed her his handkerchief. "Here, wipe your eyes. Don't let these white people see you cry." Then he took her hand again, and Amelia left it in his grasp.

As they approached the large, two-storied, white clapboard building, Amelia hoped she would soon wake up from a bad dream. Then a tall, big-boned, middle-aged woman, with a florid complexion, opened the massive front door. Sam used his best English to speak to the matron, "I heard you take in Cherokee girls here. Amelia is a good girl. She won't give you any trouble."

Amelia looked at the scary looking woman and trembled. She tightened her grip on her father's hand and closed her eyes in an attempt to remove herself from the frightening situation.

Sam whispered, "Keep your eyes open," when he noticed what she was doing.

The matron scowled and bit off her words. "Of course, no one gives me trouble, Mister Clay. I have been the matron here for over twenty years. "

Then she took her glasses from their perch on the top of her head and peered closely at Amelia. "She seems rather young. How old is the child?"

"She's six years old. Her mother died three years ago, and I can't take proper care of her."

"That seems to happen a lot in this god-forsaken place. What killed her?"

"Her heart got weak when she was expecting Amelia's little brother. Then he repeated. "Someone told me you take in Indian girls here."

"Yes, we do, but most of our girls are at least eight. However, we had a girl die last week, and there is an available bed. Amelia may take her place. You do know about the customary payment?"

"Yes, I heard. What did the girl die from?"

"The doctor said her little heart just stopped beating. He thought she probably had a weak heart, and no one knew it until it was too late."

"That's too bad. Here you go. It's not much, but with planting coming up, it's all I can spare." He handed Matron five silver dollars.

"You're right. It's not much, but it will have to do. We will expect more donations each year of her stay with us." Matron snatched the silver and grasped Amelia's trembling, brown hand in an iron grip.

Sam Clay looked into the frightened deer eyes of his youngest child and said, "I have to leave you now, my little one, my u-s-di. Soon you'll learn to be a big, smart girl."

Amelia's heart sank as she watched her father walk away. Matron pulled her along down a long, narrow dark hall. Amelia stole a look at the big white woman and decided she was a witch. As soon as her father left, the woman pocketed two of the five silver dollars and seemed to complain when she gave another white woman the remaining three silver dollars. She threw Amelia a dark warning look, as if defying her to speak. Of course, Amelia didn't. In fact, she couldn't have told any white person anything if she had the inclination because she could only speak Cherokee. Her mother had refused to speak anything else, and her father had only allowed the boys to speak the white tongue when they had white people at their home, which rarely happened.

"They will teach you at the school," he had told her once when she had asked what the whites would call her we-sa that was purring at her feet. She had forgotten to ask him about the school because he had quickly changed the subject by asking her to come with him to see a newly-born calf.

Now she knew what a white school was. It was a place where brown-skinned children were tortured by light-eyed witches. At first, she thought she would just remain silent when the witches jabbered questions at her. But when pale hands twisted her black hair until she cried out in pain, she knew she must say something to end the hurt. Amelia screamed, "Tla! Tla!" She kept on screaming over and over to get them to stop hurting her.

"The little savage is screaming 'no' at us. Child, you must learn what no means here. Sarah, tell the little fool she must never speak in Cherokee again, and tell her the penalty if she is foolish enough to do so."

A tall, slender fawn-colored girl walked over to Amelia and gently took her hand. "Little one, you must no longer speak Cherokee. If you do, you will be badly beaten. If you do not understand something that is said to you, whisper your questions to me, or if I am not with you, simply nod and smile. Watch and listen with your eyes, ears, and heart, and in time, you will come to understand the white tongue. Come to me secretly if you have questions, but never speak to me aloud in Cherokee before others, for I will not know you."

Hearing the familiar language, Amelia felt a moment of reassurance. If this Sarah would be her friend, maybe she could survive in this cold white world. But, oh, how she yearned to go back home with her father and brothers!

STANDING OUTSIDE, SAM looked at the house for a while, as if reconsidering. Then he shook his head and began striding quickly away. Sam encountered the ten-year-old John, urinating behind the wagon. "Stupid boy! Didn't I tell you not to disgrace me in front of these whites?"

John looked up in surprise and hurt from the uncustomary cuff to his ear. Then he remembered Pa sometimes acted funny when he was around whites. He hadn't been right since Ma had died. Neither had Will. Pa used to be a smiling patient man, and Will used to play with him now and then. Not anymore.

The ride home was a complete opposite of the ride to the school. On the way there, Pa had made them all laugh when he stopped the wagon to emit a high-pitched whistle, and the brown rabbit, which no one had seen except Pa, stopped dead in its tracks to listen to him. Then Amelia burst out into some loud giggles, broke the spell, and the rabbit hopped back into the underbrush. Dumb girl! He should be happy she was gone, but it sure was quiet without her. He thought about talking to Will, but one look at his older brother's dark stony face, shut his mouth. Will was handy with his fists when provoked in the slightest.

IT WAS COMPLETELY dark when they reached the clearing where their house stood. Without being asked, John and Will unhitched the tired horses, gave them their supper of oats and bran, and drew a bucket of fresh cool water to slake their thirst.

Then their father came out and said, "Don't forget the mules, boys."

Will said, "I'm goin to the outhouse. You do it."

John knew he shouldn't say anything, but he was mad at the injustice of it. "Sure is funny how you always have to go to the outhouse when there's work to be done."

Will stopped in his tracks and turned around. "Sounds like you still ain't learned your lesson about respectin your elders."

John couldn't let it go. "I respect my elders, but I don't see any elders here."

John ran when he saw Will coming toward him with murder in his eyes. Of course, it was no good. It never was. Will was twice as fast as he would ever be. He caught him by the shoulders and threw him down on the ground. Then he twisted his arm behind his back and said, "Say 'I give up because my brother is my elder, more Cherokee than me, and he will always be better than I will ever be.'"

He resisted for a minute. "No, it ain't true, and I won't say it!"

"All of it is true. I am older than you, and I am more Cherokee than you. Remember you're the one with the ugly, red white man hair? You're no good at running, playing stick ball, hunting, or anything else that counts. Most of all, you are completely useless at fighting." Then Will twisted his arm until it felt like it was breaking.

"All right! All right! I give up because my brother is my elder, he is more Cherokee, and he will always be better than I will ever be."

"Now promise you won't ever disrespect me again."

John hesitated, and Will tightened his grip again. "All right, Pa. I promise."

By the time he had finished caring for the mules, the gnawing hunger in John's stomach felt like it was going to devour him. When he came into the house, he glimpsed his father sitting in the parlor with a bottle of whiskey in front of him, reading another of his big books by the light of a small, coal oil lamp. His father often read late into the night hours, but John never knew him to use whiskey for anything but medicinal purposes, at least in front of his children. Since John hadn't eaten since early in the morning, and no supper seemed to be coming, he reached into the warming safe of their wood cook stove and found two fat biscuits left over from breakfast. Will came in, saw what he was doing, snatched one from his hand, and quickly stuffed it into his mouth. Then he went to the bedroom they shared and shut the door.

John decided that a biscuit alone wasn't enough to satisfy his hunger. He took a china plate and a can of sorghum from the cupboard, grabbed a fork from the utensil drawer, cut the biscuit into tiny pieces, and swirled the delicious bread into the sticky sweet sorghum. He sat at the big wooden kitchen table and started eating. John longed for some fresh butter, but he didn't want to go to the spring house at this time of night to get some. There might be snakes and even worse during these dark hours. He shivered when he remembered Pa's tales of Spearfinger, a frightening monster whose favorite food was the livers of young children. Spearfinger was so powerful she could take on the appearance of your father, your aunt, or even your best friend. Just when you thought you were safe, she would stab her sharp horrible finger into your body, extract your liver, and eat it in front of you while your life drained away. Then there were the witches, who, in the form of owls, would spy on and curse those they hated from the shelter of the dark woods. No, sorghum and a biscuit would do just fine. He ate his biscuit, licked the sorghum off his fingers, and ladled some water from the drinking bucket onto his hands and the sticky plate. He quickly dried the plate and his hands on the flour sack tea towel and placed the plate back into the cupboard. All this he did very quietly so that he wouldn't disturb his father and maybe get another cuff to the ear. He stole quietly to the double bed he shared with his brother and tried to go to sleep. His mind kept whirring like one of those new wind-up toys that Uncle June sent him from Texas one year.

Why did his brother hate him so much? He didn't want to hate Will, but it was hard not to when he mistreated him the way he did. John supposed he loved his sister, and he didn't know why Pa left her so far from home. His heart sank when he realized she was probably scared and crying from feeling all alone. John would miss hearing Amelia's laugh and seeing her eyes light up when he paid extra attention to her. How long would it be before he saw his little sister again? John finally fell into a deep sleep, but all night he dreamed of little Amelia being chased by Spearfinger and witches.

CPSIA information can be obtained
at www.ICGtesting.com
Printed in the USA
LVHW091935091120
671182LV00021BA/922/J

9 781633 735781